RAVELLI'S
DEFIANT BRIDE

RAVELLI'S DEFIANT BRIDE

BY

LYNNE GRAHAM

First published in Great Britain 2014
by Mills & Boon, an imprint of Harlequin (UK) Limited,
Large Print edition 2014
Eton House, 18-24 Paradise Road,
Richmond, Surrey, TW9 1SR

© 2014 Lynne Graham

ISBN: 978-0-263-24103-7

For Michael and thirty-five happy years.

CHAPTER ONE

CRISTO RAVELLI SURVEYED the family lawyer in disbelief. 'Is this an April fool joke falling out of season?' he enquired with a frown.

Robert Ludlow, senior partner of Ludlow and Ludlow, did not react with amusement. Cristo, a leading investment banker specialising in venture capital, and richer than Croesus, was not a man to be teased. Indeed, if he had a sense of humour Robert had yet to see it. Cristo, unlike his late and most probably unlamented father, Gaetano Ravelli, took life very seriously.

'I'm afraid it's not a joke,' Robert confirmed. 'Your father had five children with a woman in Ireland—'

Cristo was stunned by the concept. 'You mean, all those years he went on his fishing trips to his Irish estate—?'

'I'm afraid so. I believe the eldest child is fifteen years old—'

'*Fifteen?* But that means...' Cristo compressed his wide sensual mouth, dark eyes flaring with anger, before he could make an indiscreet comment unsuited to the ears of anyone but his brothers. He wondered why he was even surprised by yet another revelation of his father's notorious womanising. After all, throughout his irresponsible life Gaetano had left a trail of distraught and angry ex-wives and three legitimate sons in his wake, so why shouldn't there have been a less regular relationship also embellished with children?

Cristo, of course, could not answer that question because he would never ever have risked having an illegitimate child and was shaken that his father could have done so five times over. Particularly when he had never bothered to take the slightest interest in the sons he already had. Cristo's adult brothers, Nik and Zarif, would be equally astonished and appalled, but Cristo knew that the problem would fall heaviest on his own shoulders. Nik's marriage breakdown had hit him hard and his own part in that debacle still gave Cristo sleepless nights. As for their youngest sibling, as the new ruler of a country in the Middle East Zarif scarcely deserved the huge public scandal that Gaetano's immoral doings could unleash if the easily shocked media there got hold of the story.

'Fifteen years old,' Cristo mused, reflecting that Zarif's mother had evidently been betrayed throughout her entire marriage to his father without even being aware of the fact. That was not a reality that Zarif would want put out on public parade. 'I apologise for my reaction, Robert. This development comes as a considerable shock. The mother of the children—what do you know about her?'

Robert raised a greying brow. 'I contacted Daniel Petrie, the land agent of the Irish estate, and made enquiries. He said that as far as the village is concerned the woman, Mary Brophy, has long been seen as something of a disgrace and an embarrassment,' he framed almost apologetically.

'But if she was the local whore she would've been right down Gaetano's street,' Cristo breathed before he could bite back that injudicious opinion, his lean, darkly handsome face grim, but it was no secret to Gaetano's family that he had infinitely preferred bold and promiscuous women to clean-living ones. 'What provision did my father make for this horde of children?'

'That's why I decided to finally bring this matter to your attention.' Robert cleared his throat awkwardly. 'As you will be aware, Gaetano made no mention of either the woman or the children in his will.'

'Are you telling me that my father made *no* provision for these dependants?' Cristo prompted incredulously. 'He had five children with this…this woman over the course of many years and yet he settled no money on them?'

'Not so much as a penny piece on any of them…*ever*,' Robert confirmed uncomfortably.

'I thought he might have made some private arrangement to take care of them but apparently not as I have received an enquiry concerning school fees from the woman. As you know, your father always thought in terms of the present, not the future, and I imagine he assumed that he would be alive well into his eighties.'

'Instead of which he died at sixty-two years old, as foolish as ever, and tipped this mess into *my* lap,' Cristo ground out, losing all patience the more he learned of the situation. 'I'll have to look into this matter personally. I don't want the newspapers getting hold of the story—'

'Naturally not,' Robert agreed. 'It's a given that the media enjoy telling tales about men with multiple wives and mistresses.'

Well aware of that fact, Cristo clenched his even white teeth, dark eyes flaming pure gold with rage at the prospect. His father had been enough of an embarrassment while alive. He was infuriated by the idea that Gaetano might prove even more of an embarrassment after his death.

'It will be my hope that the children can be put up for adoption and this whole distasteful business quietly buried,' Cristo confided smooth as glass.

For some reason, he noted that Robert looked a little disconcerted by that idea and then the older man swiftly composed his face into blandness. 'You think the mother will agree to that?'

'If she's the usual type of woman my father favoured, she'll be glad to do as I ask for the right…compensation.' Cristo selected the word with suggestive cool.

Robert understood his meaning and tried and failed to imagine a scenario in which for the right price a woman would be willing to surrender her children for adoption. He had no doubt that Cristo had cause to know exactly what he was talking about and he was suddenly grateful not to be living a life that had made him that cynical about human nature and greed. But then, having handled Gaetano's financial dealings for years, he knew that Cristo came from a dysfunctional background and would be challenged to recognise the depth of love and loyalty that many adults cherished for their offspring.

Cristo, already stressed from his recent business trip to Switzerland, squared his broad shoulders and lifted his phone to tell his PA, Emily, to book him on a flight to Dublin. He would get this repugnant business sorted out straight away and then get straight back to work.

'I *hate* them!' Belle vented in a helpless outburst, her lovely face full of angry passion. 'I hate every Ravelli alive!'

'Then you would also have to hate your own brothers and sisters,' her grandmother reminded her wryly. 'And you know that's not how you feel—'

With difficulty, Belle mastered her hot temper and studied her grandmother apologetically. Isa was a small supple woman with iron-grey hair and level green eyes the same shade as Belle's. 'That wretched lawyer hasn't even replied to Mum's letter about the school fees yet. I hate the whole lot of them for making us beg for what should be the children's by right!'

'It's unpleasant,' Isa Kelly conceded ruefully. 'But what we have to remember is that the person responsible for this whole horrible situation is Gaetano Ravelli—'

'I'm never going to forget that!' her granddaughter swore vehemently, leaping upright in frustration to pace over to the window that overlooked the tiny back garden.

And that was certainly the truth. Belle had been remorselessly bullied at school because of her mother's relationship with Gaetano Ravelli and the children she had had with him. A lot of people had taken exception to the spectacle of a woman carrying on a long-running, *fertile* affair with a married man. Her mother, Mary, had been labelled a slut and, as a sensitive adolescent, Belle had been forced to carry the shadow of that humiliating label alongside her parent.

'He's gone now,' Isa reminded her unnecessarily. 'And so, more sadly, is your mother.'

A familiar ache stirred below Belle's breast-bone for the loss of that warm, loving presence in her family home and her angry face softened in expression. It was only a month since her mother had died from a heart attack and Belle was still not over the shock of her sudden passing. Mary had been a smiling, laughing woman in her early forties, who had rarely been ill. Yet she'd had a weak heart, and had apparently been warned by the doctor not to risk another pregnancy after the twins' difficult birth. But when had Mary Brophy ever listened to common sense? Belle asked herself painfully. Mary had gone her own sweet way regardless of the costs, choosing passion over commitment and the birth of a sixth child triumphing over what might have been years of quiet cautious living.

Whatever anyone had said about Mary Brophy—and there had been all too many local people with a moral axe to grind about her long-term affair with Gaetano—Mary had been a hardworking, kind person, who had never had a bad word to say about anyone and had always been the first to offer help when a neigh-bour was in trouble. Over the years some of her mother's most vociferous critics had ended up becoming her friends when they finally appreci-ated her gentle nature. But Belle had never been like the mother she had seen as oppressed: she had loved her mother and hated Gaetano Rav-elli for his lying, manipulative selfishness and tight-fisted ways.

As if sensing the tension in the air, Tag whined at her feet and she stretched down a hand to soothe the family dog, a small black and white Jack Russell whose big brown adoring eyes were pinned to her. Straightening again, her colourful hair spilling across her slim shoul-ders, Belle pushed a straying corkscrew curl from her Titian mane out of her strained eyes and wondered when she would find the time to get it trimmed and how on earth she would ever pay for it when money was required for far more basic necessities.

At least the Lodge at the foot of the drive winding up to Mayhill House was theirs, signed over by Gaetano years earlier to give her mother a false sense of security. But how much use was a roof over their heads when Belle still couldn't pay the bills? Even so, homelessness would have been far worse, she acknowledged ruefully, her generous mouth softening. In any case, in all likelihood she would have to sell the Lodge and find them somewhere cheaper and smaller to live. Unfortunately she was going to have to fight and fight hard for the children to receive what was rightfully theirs. Illegitimate or not, her siblings had a legal claim to a share of their late father's estate and it was her job to take on that battle for them.

'You *must* let me take charge of the children now,' Isa told her eldest granddaughter firmly. 'Mary was my daughter and she made mistakes. I don't want to stand by watching you pay the price for them—'

'The kids would be too much for you,' Belle protested, for her grandmother might be hale and hearty but she was seventy years old and

Belle thought it would be very wrong to allow her to take on such a burden.

'You attended a university miles from here to escape the situation your mother had created and you planned to go to London to work as soon as you graduated,' Isa reminded her stubbornly.

'That's the thing about life…it changes without warning you,' Belle fielded wryly. 'The children have lost both parents in the space of two months and they're very insecure. The last thing they need right now is for me to vanish as well.'

'Bruno and Donetta both go to boarding school, so they're out of the equation aside of holiday time,' the older woman reasoned, reluctant to cede the argument. 'The twins are at primary school. Only Franco is at home and he's two so he'll soon be off to school as well—'

Shortly after her mother's death, Belle had thought much along the same lines and had felt horribly guilty to admit, even to herself, that she felt trapped by the existence of her little brothers and sisters and their need for constant loving care. Her grandmother, Isa, had made her generous offer and Belle had kept it in reserve in the back of her mind, believing that it could be a real possibility. But that was before she got into the daily grind of seeing to her siblings' needs and finally appreciated the amount of sheer hard graft required and that any prospect of her grandmother taking charge was a selfish fantasy. It would be too big a burden for Isa to take on when some days it was even too much for Belle at the age of twenty-three.

Someone rapped loudly on the back door, making both women jump in surprise. Frowning, Belle opened the door and then relaxed when she saw an old friend waiting on the step. Mark Petrie and Belle had gone to school together where Mark had been one of her few true friends.

'Come in,' she invited the slimly built dark-haired man clad in casual jeans. 'Have a seat. Coffee?'

'Thanks.'

'How are you doing, Mark?' Isa asked with a welcoming smile.

'I'm doing great. It's Belle I'm worried about,' Mark admitted heavily, throwing Isa's granddaughter a look of unvarnished male admiration. 'Look, I'll just spit it right out. I heard my father talking on the phone this morning and he must've been talking to someone from Gaetano Ravelli's family. I think it was the eldest one, Cristo—'

Tensing at the sound of that familiar name, Belle settled a mug of coffee down on the table for Mark. 'Why do you think that?'

'Cristo is the executor of Gaetano's estate and my father was being asked about your mother and, of course, he doesn't even know Mary's dead yet. Nobody's bothered to tell him that she passed while he and Mum were staying with my uncle in Australia—'

'Well, your father and my mother weren't exactly bosom pals,' Belle reminded Mark bluntly. There had been a lot of bad blood over the years between the land agent, Daniel Petrie, and Mayhill's housekeeper, Mary Brophy. 'So why would anyone mention it to him?'

Cristo Ravelli, Belle was thinking resentfully. The stuffed-shirt banker and outrageously good-looking eldest son, who never ever smiled. Over the years she had often researched Gaetano's tangled love life on the Internet, initially out of curiosity but then more often to learn the answers to the questions that her poor trusting mother had never dared to ask. She knew about the wives, the sons and the scandalous affairs and had soon recognised that Gaetano was a deceitful, destructive Svengali with the female sex, who left nothing but wreckage and regrets in his wake. Furthermore, as Gaetano had only ever married *rich* women, her poor misguided mother had never had a prayer of getting him to the altar.

'The point is, evidently Ravelli's family have decided they want Gaetano's children with Mary to be adopted—'

'Adopted?' Belle interrupted, openly aston-

ished by that suggestion coming at her out of nowhere.

'Obviously the man's family want the whole affair hushed up,' Mark opined with a grimace. 'And what better way to stage a cover-up? It would keep the story out of the papers and tidy up all the loose ends—'

'But they're *not* loose ends—they're children with a family and a home!' Belle argued in dismay. 'For goodness' sake, they belong together!'

Uncomfortable in receipt of that emotional outburst, Mark cleared his throat. 'Are you the children's legal guardian?'

'Well, who else is there?' Belle asked defensively.

'But it's not down legally on paper anywhere that you're their guardian, is it?' Mark prompted ruefully as her clear green eyes lifted to his in sudden dismay. 'I didn't think so. You should go and see a solicitor about your situation as soon as you can and get your claim to the children recognised with all the red tape available…otherwise you might discover that Gaetano's family have more legal say on the subject of what happens to them than you do.'

'But that would be ridiculous!' Belle objected. 'Gaetano had nothing to do with the kids even when he was here.'

'Not according to the law. He paid the older children's school fees, signed the Lodge over to your mother,' Mark reminded her with all the devotion to detail inherent in his law-student studies. 'He may have been a lousy father in the flesh but he did take care of the necessities, which could conceivably give Gaetano's sons a bigger say than you have in what happens to the children now.'

'But Gaetano left all five of them *out* of his will,' Belle pointed out, tilting her chin in challenge.

'That doesn't matter. The law is the law,' Mark fielded. 'Nobody can take their birthright away from them.'

'Adoption…' Eyes still stunned by that proposition, Belle sank heavily back down into her chair. 'That's a crazy idea. They couldn't have tried this nonsense on if my mother were still alive!' she exclaimed bitterly. 'Nobody could have said their mother didn't have the right to say what should happen to them.'

'If only Mary had lived long enough to deal with all this,' Isa sighed in pained agreement. 'But maybe, as the children's granny, I'll have a say?'

'I doubt it,' Mark interposed. 'Until you moved in here after Mary's death, the children had never lived with you.'

'I could pretend to be Mum...' Belle breathed abruptly.

'*Pretend*?' Isa's head swivelled round to the younger woman in disbelief. 'Don't be silly, Belle.'

'How am I being silly? Cristo Ravelli doesn't know Mum is dead and if he thinks she's still alive, he's very unlikely to try and interfere in their living arrangements.' Belle lifted her head high, convinced she was correct on that score.

'There's no way you could pretend to be a

woman in her forties!' Mark protested with an embarrassed laugh at the idea.

Belle was thinking hard. 'But I don't need to look like I'm in my forties…I only need to look old enough to have a fifteen-year-old son and, at the age women are having children these days, I could easily only be in my early thirties,' she reasoned.

'It would be insane to try and pull off a deception like that,' her grandmother told her quellingly. 'Cristo Ravelli would be sure to find out the truth.'

'*How?* Who's going to tell him? He's a Ravelli—he's not going to be wandering round asking the locals nosy questions. He would have no reason to question my identity. I'll put my hair up, use a lot of make-up…that'll help—'

'Belle…I know you're game for anything but it would be a massive deception to try and pull off,' Mark said drily. 'Think about what you're saying.'

The kitchen door opened and a thumb-sucking toddler with a mop of black curls stumbled in. He steadied himself against Belle's denim-clad thigh and then clambered up clumsily into his sister's lap, taking his welcome for granted. 'Sleepy,' he told her, the words slurring. 'Hug…'

Belle cradled her youngest half-sibling gently. Franco was very affectionate and he was quick to curve his warm, solid little body into hers. 'I'll take him upstairs for a nap,' she whispered, rising upright again with difficulty because he was a heavy child.

Belle tucked Franco into his cot beside her bed and for a moment stood looking out of the rear window, which provided a picturesque view of Mayhill House, a gracious grey Georgian mansion set in acres of parkland against the backdrop of the ancient oak woods. Her mother had been a widow and Belle only eight years old when Mary had first started work as Gaetano Ravelli's housekeeper.

Belle's own father had been a violent drunk, renowned for his foul-mouthed harangues and propensity for getting into fights. One night he had stepped out in front of a car when under the influence and few had mourned his demise, least of all Belle, who had been terrified of her father's vicious temper and brutal fists. Mother and daughter had believed they were embarking on a new and promising life when Mary became the Mayhill housekeeper. Sadly, however, Mary had fallen madly in love with her new boss and her reputation had been destroyed from the instant Belle's eldest half-sibling, Bruno, had been born.

Someone like Cristo Ravelli, Belle reflected bitterly, could have absolutely no grasp of how other less fortunate mortals lived. Cristo was handsome, brilliant and obscenely successful. He had grown up in a golden cocoon of cash, the son of a very wealthy Italian princess who was renowned as a leading society hostess. His stepfather was a Hungarian banker, his home a Venetian palace and he had attended an exclusive school from which he had emerged literally weighed down with academic and athletic honours. It was hardly surprising that Cristo was a dazzling star of success in every corner of his life. After all, *he* didn't know what it was to be humiliated, ignored or mocked and she'd bet he had never had to apologise for his parentage.

On the other hand Bruno had only been thirteen when Gaetano first accused his son of being gay because that was the only way Gaetano could interpret Bruno's burning desire to be an artist. Belle's little brother had been devastated by that destructive indictment from a father whom he had long been desperate to impress. His growing unhappiness at school where he was being bullied had resulted in a suicide attempt. Belle still got the shivers recalling it, having come so terrifyingly close to losing her little brother for ever. Bruno *needed* his family for support. Bruno, just like his siblings, needed love and commitment to grow into a contented, well-adjusted adult. There was nothing Belle would not have done to ensure that her siblings remained happy and together.

Having delivered his warning, Mark was taking his leave when she returned downstairs.

'I'll get supper on,' Belle's grandmother declared.

'You're not serious about trying to pretend to be Mary, are you?' Mark pressed on the doorstep.

Belle straightened her slight shoulders. 'If that's what it takes to keep the family together, I'd do it in a heartbeat!'

The evening light was fast fading when Cristo's car finally turned up the long driveway to Mayhill.

He had never visited Gaetano's Irish bolt hole before because Gaetano had never invited any of his relatives to visit him there or, indeed, anywhere else. His father had never bothered to maintain relationships and the minute he was bored he had headed for pastures new and wiped the slate clean of past associations.

A woman with a little dog running at her heels was walking across the sweeping front lawn. Cristo frowned; he didn't like trespassers. But a split second later he was staring, watching that cloud of colourful curls float back from a stunning heart-shaped face, noting the way her loose top blew back to frame her lush full breasts and a sliver of pale flat stomach, exposing the denim shorts that hugged her derriere and accentuated her long, long shapely legs. She took his breath away and the pulse at his groin reacted with rampant enthusiasm. He gritted his teeth, trying to recall when he had last been with a woman, and when he couldn't blamed that oversight for his sudden arousal. In reality, Cristo always chose work over sex for work challenged and energised him while he regarded sex as a purely stress-relieving exercise.

He unlocked the massive wooden front door and stepped over the top of a pile of untouched post into a large black-and-white-tiled hall. His protection team composed of Rafe and John moved past him. 'We'll check the house.'

A fine layer of dust coated the furniture within view and Cristo was not surprised when Rafe confirmed that the house was vacant. But then, what exactly had he expected? Mary Brophy and her five children occupying the property? Yes, that was *exactly* what he had expected and why he had used his keys to emphasise the fact that he had the right of entry. He strode through the silent rooms, eventually ending up in the kitchen with its empty fridge standing wide open, backed by the sound of a dripping tap. His handsome mouth curved down as he noted the phone on the wall. One of the buttons was labelled 'housekeeping'. Lifting the phone, he stabbed the button with exasperated force.

'Yes?' a disembodied female voice responded when he had almost given up hope of his call being answered.

'It's Cristo Ravelli. I'm at the house. Why hasn't it been prepared for my arrival?' he demanded imperiously.

At the other end of the phone, Belle went on all systems alert at the vibrating tone of impatience in that dark, deep accented drawl and her green eyes suddenly glinted as dangerously as emeralds in firelight. 'Do you think maybe that could be because the housekeeper's wages were stopped the same day Mr Ravelli crashed his helicopter?'

Cristo was not accustomed to smart-mouthed replies and his wide sensual mouth hardened. 'I didn't make that instruction.'

'Well, it doesn't really matter now, does it? Regrettably nobody works for free,' Belle told him drily.

Cristo bit back a curse. He was tired and hungry and in no mood for a war of words. 'I gather you're the housekeeper?'

It was the moment of truth, Belle registered, and for a split second she hesitated. An image of her siblings rehomed in an orphanage on the slippery slope to a foster home gripped her tummy and provoked nausea. 'Er…yes,' she pronounced tightly.

'Then get yourself up to the house and do your job. I can assure you that you will be well paid for your time,' Cristo informed her grittily. 'I need food and bedding—'

'There's several shops in the village. You

must've driven past them to get to the house,' Belle protested.

'I'm happy to pay you to take care of those tasks for me,' Cristo fielded smoothly before returning the phone to the wall and wondering if it had been wise to recall an insolent house-keeper to her former duties. Reminding himself that he only planned to stay a couple of days before arranging to have the house sold, he dis-missed the matter from mind. The housekeeper, he reflected, would be a useful source of local knowledge to have on hand.

Following that call, Belle was in an infinitely more excitable state. After all, it was now or never. She couldn't introduce herself as Mary's daughter and then change her mind. Either she pretended to be her mother or she went up to Mayhill and told Cristo Ravelli that his father's former housekeeper/lover was dead. But when she thought of the influence she could poten-tially wield for the children's benefit by acting as their mother, her doubts fell away and she hurried upstairs, frantically wondering how she could best make herself look more mature.

The first thing she did was take off her shorts and top. Rustling through her wardrobe, she found a short stretchy skirt and a long-sleeved tee. Her mother had never ever worn flat heels or jeans and Belle owned only one skirt. Clinging to those Mary Brophy habits as if they might prove to be a good-luck talisman, Belle pulled out a pair of high heels and hurriedly got dressed. That achieved, she went into the bathroom, pushed her hair back from her face and grimaced at her porcelain-pale complexion, which she had often suspected made her look even younger than her years. Surely if she put her hair up and went heavy on the make-up it would make her look older? Brows pleating, she recalled the smoky eye treatment that a friend had persuaded her to try on a night out and she dug deep into her make-up bag for the necessary tools.

She stroked on the different shadows with a liberal hand, blurred the edges with an anxious fingertip and added heaps of eyeliner. Well, she certainly looked different, she acknowledged uneasily, layering on the mascara before adding blush to her cheeks and outlining her mouth with bright pink gloss.

'I was about to call you down for supper...' Isa Kelly froze in the tiny hall to watch her granddaughter come downstairs. 'Where on earth are you going got up like that?'

Belle stiffened. 'Why? Do I look odd?'

'Well, if you bent over you could probably treat me to a view of your underwear,' Isa commented disapprovingly.

An awkward silence fell, interrupted within seconds by the noisy sound of the back door opening and closing. Children's voices raised in shrill argument broke the silence and a dark-haired boy and girl of eight years of age hurtled into the hall still engaged in hurling insults.

'If you don't stop fighting, it will be early to bed tonight,' Belle warned the twins, Pietro and Lucia.

The twins closed their mouths, ducked their

tousled heads and surged up the stairs past their eldest sister.

'You can tell me now why you're wearing a skirt,' Isa pressed Belle.

'Cristo Ravelli phoned…in need of a house-keeper.' Belle quickly explained what had transpired on the phone. 'I need to look at least ten years older.'

As Belle spoke, Isa studied the younger woman in consternation. 'You can't possibly pretend to be Mary… It's an insane idea. You'll never get away with it.'

Belle lifted her chin. 'But it's worth a try if it means that Cristo Ravelli has to listen to what I have to say. He obviously knows nothing about Mum. I don't think he even realises that she was his father's housekeeper.'

'I doubt if he's that ignorant,' Isa opined thoughtfully. 'It could be a shrewd move. Naturally he's going to want to meet the children's mother as soon as possible. But I don't want you going up there to run after the man, doing his shopping and cooking and making up his bed, especially dressed like that!'

'What's wrong with the way I'm dressed?'

'It might give the man the wrong idea.'

'I seriously doubt that,' Belle responded, smoothing her stretchy skirt carefully down over her slim hips. 'As far as I'm aware he's not sex-mad like his father.'

Isa compressed her lips. 'That kind of comment is *so* disrespectful, Belle.'

'It's a fact, not a nasty rumour.'

'Gaetano was the children's father. He may not have been much of a father but you still shouldn't talk about him like that where you could be overheard,' her grandmother rebuked her firmly.

Aware that the older woman was making a fair point, Belle reddened with discomfiture. 'May I borrow your car, Gran?'

'Yes, of course.' Belatedly aware that Belle had successfully sidetracked her concern about the deception she was preparing to spring on Cristo Ravelli, Isa planted a staying hand on the front door before Belle could open it. 'Think about what you're about to do, Belle. Once you try to deceive this man, there's no going back and he'll have every right to be very angry with us all when he discovers the truth…as eventually he must,' she reasoned anxiously.

'Cristo is a Ravelli, Gran…shrewd, tricky and unscrupulous. I need an advantage to deal with him and the only way I can get that advantage is by pretending to be Mum.'

CHAPTER TWO

BELLE DROVE DOWN to the garage shop in the village to stock up on basic necessities for the Mayhill kitchen and was taken aback by the cost of the exercise.

Cristo Ravelli was expecting her to cook but she couldn't cook, at least not anything that required more than a microwave and a tin opener. She pondered her dilemma and decided on an omelette, salad and garlic bread. Surely even she could manage a meal that basic? She had often watched her mother and her grandmother making omelettes. Bruno was also a dab hand in the kitchen. They always ate well when he was home at weekends.

Tense as a steel girder, she drove round to the back of the house, noting that the lights weren't on. The back door was still locked and with a groan she lugged her carrier bags round to the front, mounted the steps and pressed the doorbell.

Cristo was on the phone when the bell echoed through the hall. Brows drawing together, he went to answer the door, stepping back in surprise when a slender redhead in sky-high heels tramped in past him. The housekeeper? Not his idea of a housekeeper, he conceded, swiftly concluding his call, his brilliant dark eyes flaring over one of the shapeliest bodies he had ever seen and very probably the best ever legs. Legs that put him in mind of the girl he had seen walking across the lawn, his gaze rising to the woman's face to note the huge anxious green eyes lost in the heavy make-up and the ripe full mouth. She was not his type, no way was she his type, too obvious, too loud, hair too red. Indeed Cristo knew to his cost that he was most attracted to tiny ice-cool blondes with big blue eyes. His conscience sliced through that thought instantaneously, reminding him that that particular image was forbidden for very good reasons. Lush black lashes shielding his grim and

guilty gaze, he rested his attention quite deliberately on the redhead's remarkable breasts. Now,
those were truly a work of art like her legs, he
conceded abstractedly.

Sadly accustomed to the effect her full bosom
tended to have on the male sex, Belle studied
Cristo Ravelli at her leisure. By any estimate,
he was drop-dead gorgeous. He had luxuriant
black hair closely cropped to his arrogant head,
spectacular bone structure and quite stunning
dark-as-charcoal eyes enhanced by absurdly
long sooty lashes. A light shadow of stubble
roughened his olive-skinned jaw line, adding to
an already overpoweringly masculine presence.

Her pupils dilated, her heart began hammering an upbeat tempo and her tummy performed
acrobatics. It was nerves, she told herself, nerves
and adrenalin reacting to the challenge of the
deception she was embarking on. It didn't help
that Cristo was also extremely tall, actually tall
enough to make her feel small even though she
was an easy five feet eight inches in height and
stood even higher in heels. His shoulders were

broad below the tailored jacket of his no doubt expensive business suit, his chest wide, his lean hips tapering down to legs that were very long and powerful.

'I'll take these down to the kitchen and start cooking,' Belle told him, raising her arms to display the bulging carrier bags.

Her rounded breasts shimmied below the fine jersey top and Cristo's mouth ran dry. 'You're my father's housekeeper?' he prompted because she was not at all what he had expected, having dimly imagined some feisty but sensible coun- trywoman of indeterminate age.

Abandoning her attempt to walk right by him, Belle set the bags on the floor at her feet and lifted her head high. 'I'm Mary Brophy,' she announced, thrusting up her chin in challenge.

Both disconcertion and disbelief assailed Cristo and his dark deep-set eyes narrowed to increase their searching intensity as he scruti- nised her. 'You were my father's...mistress?' he asked.

Nausea stirred in her tummy at that label but

she could think of no more accurate description for the compromising position her late mother had occupied in Gaetano's life and colour fired her cheeks. 'Yes.'

A split second earlier, Cristo had been mentally undressing her and that awareness now revolted him as the ultimate in inappropriate activities now that he knew who she was. This was the woman who had occupied his father's bed for at least fifteen years, earning a longevity that no other women had contrived to match in Gaetano's easily bored existence. And looking at her, suddenly Cristo was not surprised by that fact because self-evidently this woman worked at her appearance. Even after giving birth to five children she still had the slender waist of a young girl and, below the make-up she seemed to trowel on as thick as paste, her fine pale skin was unlined and still taut. She was too young, way too young-looking though to match the woman he had expected to meet, he decided, his ebony brows pleating in perplexity.

'You were also Gaetano's housekeeper?' Cristo questioned.

'Yes.' With determination, Belle bent down to lift the bags again. 'Omelette and salad all right for you?' she asked, heading for the kitchen at speed.

A very decorative housekeeper, Cristo thought numbly, still quite unable to picture her as the mother of five children. *Five!*

'You must have been very young when you met my father,' Cristo commented from the kitchen doorway.

Belle stiffened as she piled the perishable food into the fridge. 'Not that young,' she fielded, wanting to tell him to mind his own business but reluctant to cause offence. After all, she needed his support to secure a decent future for her siblings. Although what realistic chance did she have of gaining it? At worst, Cristo Ravelli might despise and resent his father's illegitimate children, and at best, he might be simply indifferent to them. Adoption, for goodness' sake, she reflected in lingering disbelief. How many people would even *dare* to suggest such an option?

'I assumed you would be living here in the house,' Cristo remarked, his attention clinging of its own volition to the amount of slender thigh on view as she crouched down to pack the fridge.

'I only…er…lived in when Gaetano was here,' Belle said awkwardly.

'And the rest of the time?' Cristo enquired, because as far as he knew his father had only come to Ireland three or four times a year and had never stayed for longer than a couple of weeks at most.

'I live in the lodge at the gates,' Belle admitted grudgingly, straightening to set out lettuce and eggs on the granite work counter.

Cristo gritted his teeth at the news because she and her children would have to vacate the lodge house before he could put Mayhill on the market. Of course he would have to pay her for the inconvenience of finding another home. Her hair shone bright as a beacon below the lights, displaying varying shades of gold, auburn and copper, tiny curls of hair adorning the nape of her long, elegant neck. She had very curly hair, the sort of hair he had once seen on a rag doll, he mused absently, irritated by the random nature of the thought. He studied the smooth line of her jaw and the full lush softness of her bold red-painted mouth with a persistent sense of incredulity. She had to be a lot older than she looked to be the parent of a teenager, although perhaps he was being naïve. It was perfectly possible that Mary Brophy looked so amazingly youthful because his father had paid for her to have plastic surgery.

Belle unwrapped the garlic bread and shoved it on an oven tray to cook. She wished he would go away. Standing there, all looming six feet four inches or so of him, he made her feel nervous and clumsy. She had to search through cupboards to find the utensils she wanted because she had rarely visited Mayhill since childhood. Indeed she had avoided it on principle whenever Gaetano was in residence. Her green eyes darkened as she recalled the way she and her ever-growing band of siblings would go and stay with her grandmother in the village even before Gaetano arrived, leaving her mother free to make her preparations for his arrival. Mary had always, *always* put Gaetano Ravelli first.

Belle remembered her mother's excitement when Gaetano was due to arrive, the frantic exercising, hair appointments and shopping trips to ensure that Mary could look her very best for her lover. Belle had long since decided that she would rather die than want to please any man to that extent. Certainly Mary's rather pathetic loyalty and devotion had not won her any prizes.

Belle prepared the salad quickly, heaping it into a bowl and then making up her mother's favourite salad dressing as best she could because she couldn't quite recall the proportions of the different ingredients. That achieved, she embarked on the omelette. Cristo had vanished by then and she heaved a sigh of relief as she walked through to set the table in the spacious dining room across the hall.

He had accepted that she was Mary Brophy without protest and why shouldn't he? It meant nothing to him that her poor mother was gone. Mark's father, the land agent Daniel Petrie, would eventually catch up on the local gossip and learn that the woman he had long despised was dead and buried. But Belle thought it was unlikely that Daniel would bother making an announcement of that fact to Cristo Ravelli as, not only would he feel foolish about having misinformed his employer, but he would also most likely assume that Cristo had already found out the truth. Soothing herself with such reflections, Belle returned to her cooking and struggled to control the gas burners because she was accustomed to cooking with electric.

Cristo surveyed his meal with an appetite that very quickly vanished. He prodded the omelette with a fork. It had the solid consistency of a rubber mattress but lacked the bounce. The salad had been drowned in a vat of oil. Even the garlic bread was charred although valiant attempts had been made to cut away the most burnt bits. He swallowed hard and pushed the plate away. She couldn't cook, but presumably she and his father had dined out. Distaste suddenly filled Cristo and he stood up in a lithe movement, his lean strong face hard and taut. He didn't want to be in Ireland. He didn't want to deal with the wretched woman and the consequences of her sordid long-term affair with his father. But he knew that he didn't have a choice. Mary Brophy and her children were not a problem he could afford to ignore. In any case, there was no one else to deal with the situation.

Belle was digging into the linen cupboard on the upper landing when she heard a noise behind her and whirled round to stare in dismay at the tall square-featured young man leaning back against the bannister. He was built like a solid brick wall.

'So this is where the bedding is hidden,' he remarked.

'Who are you?' Belle demanded nervously.

'Rafe is one of my two bodyguards,' Cristo

interposed, strolling up onto the landing. 'Rafe and John are staying here with me.'

'John and I need bedding. We can take care of ourselves though,' Rafe declared, stepping past her to peruse the tidy, labelled shelves just as she emerged clutching the linen she required for the master bedroom. Conscious of Cristo Ravelli's stare, and feeling somewhat harassed, Belle walked stiffly down the corridor. Damn the man! Why was he watching her like that? Did she have two heads all of a sudden? And why hadn't he told her he had companions? She hadn't bought enough food and that thought reminded her that she had to get him to settle up with her for the shopping she had done on his behalf. Dropping the linen on the bed, she dug into her pocket for the till receipt and turned to offer it to him.

'This is what you owe me,' she told him.

Cristo dug out his wallet and extended a banknote while still engaged in frowning at the gilded furniture and mirrors and the fantastically draped red king-size bed. 'Is this my father's room?'

'Yes.'

'I'll sleep somewhere else. The Victorian brothel design doesn't appeal to me,' he informed her curtly.

The décor was dark, fussy and horrible, Belle was willing to concede. She lifted the linen again and trudged across the corridor to one of the few guest rooms that enjoyed an en suite. Mayhill was badly in need of updating.

'When I said that about the decoration, I didn't intend to insult you,' Cristo remarked, standing poised by the window, thinking that at this early stage it would be most unwise to offend her. He swore to himself that he would make no cheap cracks about her role as his father's mistress, not least because it was becoming clear that it had not been a profitable position, he reflected wryly, which was hardly surprising when Gaetano had been renowned for his stinginess. Indeed in every one of his three divorces Gaetano had made money off his ex-wives in spite of the fact that in each case the women had been the injured parties. That Gaetano's secret mistress had still been working as his house-keeper and wore cheap off-the-peg clothing should really not come as a surprise. For that reason he found it hard to believe that Gaetano had stumped up for plastic surgery to keep his mistress looking young but, of course, he re-minded himself, it was perfectly possible that there had been no cosmetic enhancement. Mary Brophy could simply be, and probably was, a very lucky woman who looked much younger than her years.

'I'm not offended. I wasn't involved in choos-ing the furnishings here. About ten years ago, Gaetano hired an interior decorator,' Belle ex-plained, recalling how very hurt her mother had been not to be trusted with that responsibility by her lover. But then good taste had not been her mother's strong point either. The Lodge re-joiced in every shade of pink known to man, pink having been Mary's favourite colour.

Cristo watched Belle crush the pillows into

pillow slips, her slender figure twisting this way and that, allowing him to notice her ripe, pouting curves at breast and hip from every angle. His wide sensual mouth slowly settled into a harder and harder line as he studied her delicate flushed profile, scanning her fine brows, her subtle little nose and full pink mouth. And his body reacted accordingly, stirring with forbidden interest until he angrily turned his back on her, castigating himself for viewing his father's mistress as if she were some kind of sex object. But then he reminded himself that she was dressed to attract in an outfit and shoes that accentuated her long legs and shapely figure, and, when all was said and done, he was still a man with all that entailed and almost guaranteed to look.

Belle shot a sidewise glance at Cristo from below her lashes. His detachment, his air of command and superiority reminded her of his father, who had barely acknowledged Belle's existence on the rare occasions when he had seen her. Suddenly she regretted agreeing to play housekeeper because no doubt as intended it made her feel inferior. Her soft mouth tightened as she shook out the duvet with unnecessary violence and then carried the towels into the bathroom. Unfortunately she carried the image of Cristo Ravelli with her, those penetrating eyes dark as sin, that sleek bred-in-the-bone sexiness that lent him such charismatic appeal. She could feel her nipples pushing hard against the scratchy surface of her lace bra, a tightening, sliding sensation of warmth between her thighs and she was deeply disturbed by her reaction. But there was no denying it: *he* appealed to her; *he* attracted her on the most basic level. Did that mean that at heart she was as foolish as her mother had once been about Gaetano?

'I'd appreciate the opportunity to have a private word with you here tomorrow morning,' Cristo murmured smoothly as she emerged again. 'Shall we say at ten?'

Belle nodded agreement. 'When will you want to meet the children?' she prompted.

Cristo froze, his facial bones locking tight. 'I

don't…wish to meet them, that is,' he extended unapologetically, dark eyes cold as black ice.

Belle paled, uncertain of how to take that statement. Was his lack of interest good or bad news for her siblings? Did that mean that the adoption idea was just a silly rumour? She scrutinised his lean, handsome features with frowning green eyes, unnerved by his icy reserve and lack of humanity. Did he think nothing of the blood tie? A lot of people would just have agreed to meet the children for the sake of it, even if they weren't particularly interested in them, but Cristo Ravelli had chosen to spurn even that polite pretence.

In acknowledging that, Belle felt sheer loathing suddenly leap through her in a fierce wave of antagonism because she was gutted on her siblings' behalf by his detachment. Was he refusing to accept that the children were part of the Ravelli family? *Obviously.* Clearly, Mary Brophy's children were not good enough to make the grade, just as Mary had never been good enough for Gaetano to marry. Bile scoured

Belle's throat as she sped downstairs to clean up the kitchen and go home. She hoped he wasn't expecting her to come up and cook breakfast when she found the meal she had cooked thrown in its entirety into the bin. Her face burned but her chin came up. So, it hadn't been one of her best efforts but in her opinion it had been as much as he deserved!

After spending half the summer with Mary over twenty years earlier, Gaetano had confided that he was unhappily unmarried and Mary's hopes of a happy ending for her romance had risen high. But Gaetano had not asked his Arabic wife for a divorce or even a separation. Over the years the media had published several stories about his extramarital affairs. Her mother had refused to believe the stories, even after Belle had shown her revealing pictures on the Internet. Mary had always been very quick to make excuses in Gaetano's defence.

'He feels trapped and lonely in his marriage. It's only a business arrangement. She was a friend for years before he married her and he doesn't love her. He needed a hostess to entertain his business colleagues and she comes from an old-fashioned country where a woman needs a husband if she wants any freedom,' Mary had reasoned. 'I can't hold his marriage against him, Belle. I'm not even an educated woman. I couldn't do what his princess can do for him.'

Mary Brophy had been hopelessly infatuated with Gaetano Ravelli from the moment she first met him and she had allowed nothing to interfere with her rosy view of their relationship. Her grief in the wake of the helicopter crash that had taken Gaetano's life had been all-consuming.

'I know you don't understand,' she had said to Belle, 'but Gaetano was the love of my life. I know he wasn't interested in marrying me but nothing's perfect. I wasn't his match in money or background and I can't blame him for that. When you love someone, Belle, you accept their flaws and he was too much of a snob to want to marry an ordinary woman like me.'

A woman like me, Belle recalled painfully. It was little wonder that Mary had suffered from low self-esteem. She had travelled from a shotgun wedding at the age of seventeen straight into an abusive marriage and had finally ended up as a married man's mistress. Life had always been tough for her mother, but then, as Isa was prone to reminding Belle, Mary had *always* made the wrong choices when it came to the men in her life.

Isa was waiting up for Belle when she got back to the Lodge.

'Well?' her grandmother pressed. 'Did he actually credit the idea that you were a woman in her forties?'

'No, he assumed I must have got involved with his father when I was very young,' Belle advanced with a dismissive toss of her head. 'He did do a lot of staring, though. He's invited me up to the house to talk to him tomorrow at ten, so presumably the kids' future will be discussed then.'

The older woman released a heavy sigh. 'I

don't like the way you're going about this, Belle. Honesty is always the best policy.'

'But I won't be dealing with a nice, honest guy.'

'You hated Gaetano. Don't take it out on his son.'

Belle folded her lips at that unwelcome advice. 'He doesn't even want to meet the kids.'

Her grandmother shook her greying head, her unhappiness at that news palpable. 'If only your mother had thought about what she was doing and how much the children would be resented by the rest of Gaetano's family.'

Cristo had a troubled night of sleep. He dreamt that he was pursuing a woman with the longest legs possible across a misty landscape. Every time he got close she pulled away and laughed and her resistance made him want her more than ever, lust pounding through his veins like an explosive charge. But when he finally caught up with her, she was a different woman, pale blonde hair falling back from her piquant face to highlight big blue enquiring eyes and instantaneous recoil wakened him. He had broken out in a cold sweat, angry frustration and guilt slicing through him for the one woman he couldn't enjoy having even in his dreams…Betsy, his brother Nik's estranged wife. His jawline rigid, Cristo sprang out of bed and went for a shower.

His eyes closed tight shut below the refreshing blast of the power shower. He hadn't meant to wreck his brother's marriage. There had been no intent on his part to inflict damage, he reasoned painfully. Betsy had come to him for support, devastated by what she had learned from Zarif. But, unhappily, it had been Cristo who first gave Zarif the destructive news that had ruined Nik's relationship with his wife. Cristo had broken his brother's confidence and spoken out of turn, but he had never ever at any stage planned to harm Nik or hoped to steal Betsy from him.

For his own benefit, however, he listed the sins he had committed. He *had* thought that Nik didn't deserve a woman like Betsy. He *had* stood by watching while his brother took his wife for granted and he had *not* warned him of what he was doing. With the basest disloyalty, he *had* cherished feelings for his brother's wife. That was why Gaetano's mess in Ireland was *his* mess to clean up, Cristo reflected grimly. Nik already had enough on his plate to deal with and Zarif was still suffering the fallout from the loose-tongued confession that had wrecked Nik's marriage because ever since then the three brothers had barely spoken to each other.

'Very mumsy,' Isa pronounced the next morning with a raised brow when she saw what Belle was wearing. 'Did that skirt belong to your mother?'

Belle paled. 'Yes, I kept a couple of things just to remember Mum by. It's a little big but it looks all right with the belt.'

'Which is more than you can say about that flapping cardigan and the beads round your neck with that fussy blouse,' Isa groaned disapprovingly. 'You look like a young woman trying to look older.'

'Yes but that's because you know the truth. It's daylight now and I need to make a better impression than I did last night,' Belle pointed out anxiously.

'Even daylight couldn't penetrate the amount of make-up you've got on,' her grandmother said drily. 'But you're right—it does age you.'

'Look, I accept that Cristo is eventually going to find out the truth but I want that adoption idea off the table first,' Belle told her.

'Even at the cost of infuriating him?' Isa asked. 'Gaetano had a very low threshold for provocation.'

'Whatever happens, I'll deal with it.'

'I can't see how,' Isa said bluntly. 'You're pretty much powerless up against his wealth and intellect.'

Belle trudged up the drive in her high heels, striving not to feel like someone got up in fancy dress. She was *not* powerless. Money wasn't everything, nor was intellect. She was not stupid. She had a first-class degree in business and economics and she had the power of the unexpected on her side. He thought she was who she had said she was and, whether he knew it or not, that meant he would be fighting with one hand tied behind his back. Where her mother would have rolled over on command for a Ravelli and said thank you very much for the attention, Belle was programmed to fight dirty.

Cristo watched her approach from the window in the drawing room. No miniskirt in evidence today, but high-heeled court shoes with pointy toes embellished those award-winning legs. He gritted his even white teeth together, stamping out that inappropriate thought. So, she was an attractive woman. It was par for the course: his father's lovers had always been beauties even while his wives were more of the plain variety. Gaetano had always rated wealth and class above looks. Cristo wondered how much money it would take to persuade the older woman into his way of thinking. He was a skilled negotiator and envisaged few problems because Mary

Brophy had not been enriched in any way by her relationship with his father and was currently penniless. Furthermore she couldn't be the brightest star in the firmament when she had given the wily older man five children he could never have wanted and kept on slogging away for him as a humble housekeeper.

Surprisingly a rare shard of pity stabbed Cristo at that acknowledgement, making him register that where Mary Brophy was concerned he didn't want to use a sledgehammer to crack a nut. He didn't want to threaten or intimidate her into doing his bidding; he simply wanted a neat and tidy solution to a very messy and potentially embarrassing problem for *all* their sakes.

CHAPTER THREE

'MR RAVELLI IS in the drawing room,' Rafe informed her.

Breathing in deeply and slowly to maintain her calm front, Belle walked into the over-furnished room where the ornate drapes and blinds cut out much of the daylight. Cristo swung round to study her and instantly her every sense went on high alert, her backbone stiffening, her slim legs bracing, her soft pink lips parting as she dragged in a sudden extra shot of oxygen.

Cristo scanned her appearance, his nostrils flaring with sudden impatience. She was dressed in a frumpy skirt and cardigan that a maiden aunt might have worn and she had inexplicably teamed that look with the kind of bold make-up a streetwalker might have flaunted like a signpost. And he realised then that there was something he wasn't seeing, something he wasn't grasping about this woman, because so far her long-term affair with his father wasn't adding up at all. Whatever else might have been said about Gaetano, he had been a connoisseur of women and a sophisticate and there was no way his father had returned again and again to Ireland in order to take advantage of the charms of the woman currently standing in front of him.

'Mr Ravelli...' she said breathily and she turned her head away to glance out of the window, her hair a sunburst of colour, her fine profile delineated against the light, soft, glossy mouth full and pouting peach pink, long lashes fluttering up on big eyes as green and verdant as Irish grass.

And Cristo ground his perfect white teeth together on the smoulderingly sexual pull of her in that instant, recognising that she had buckets of that inexpressible quality that reduced the male mind to mush and turned a man on hard and fast. For a split second, he wanted to snatch her up into his arms and crush every line of the remarkable body concealed by the unattractive clothing to his own while he discovered if that voluptuous mouth of hers tasted as impossibly good as it looked. His hands closed into fists of restraint while he fought off the erection threatening, struggling to think of something, *anything*, that would take his thoughts off her mouth and her breasts and her legs and, even worse, what lay between them. That she could be affecting him on such a level outraged his every principle.

Trying to avoid direct contact with those spectacular dark-as-night eyes of his, Belle could feel her colour heightening, awareness of him leaping and pounding through her in an uncontrollable surge. She stared at him, breathless, frozen like someone cornered by a wild animal, and all the time she was noticing things about him: the way his sleek ebony brows defined his eyes, the way the faint line of colour accentuated the hard masculine angle of his high cheekbones, the way the pared-down hollows below enhanced his wide, sensual mouth. Very, very good-looking but, yes, she had noticed that

before, certainly didn't need to keep *on* noticing it. The atmosphere thickened and the silence screamed at her nerves as every muscle
in her body tightened defensively. It was as if
there were nobody else in the world but them
and what she was feeling: the insidious warmth
blossoming in her pelvis, the sudden tightening
discomfort of her nipples.

Lean, strong face rigid, Cristo expelled his
breath in a sudden hiss and took a measured
step back from her and away from such treacherous ruminations as to what she might *taste*
like, what her skin would *feel* and smell like. He
was appalled that she could drag such a strong
physical reaction from him against his will, but
even more annoyed that she could somehow
cloud his usual crystal-clear clarity of thought.

'Miss Brophy.'

'It's Mrs actually.'

Cristo frowned. 'You're married?'

'I've been a widow for many years,' Belle replied tightly, straying over to the window, par-
tially turning her back to him while she fought

to regain her mental focus. The deception she had entered on demanded her whole concentration. She was Mary Brophy, Gaetano's former mistress and the mother of five of his children, she reminded herself doggedly.

'I invited you here today to discuss your future and your children's,' Cristo delivered smoothly.

Lifted by that solid assurance, Belle's spirits perked up. 'Yes…Gaetano has left us in a pretty awkward position.'

'Naturally, you're referring to your financial situation. My father was most remiss in not making provision for you in the event of his death.'

'Yes…but he *did* sign the house over to me,' Belle pointed out, keen to sound like a loyal woman in Gaetano's defence because she could not afford to let an ounce of her loathing for the man betray her true identity in his son's presence.

Cristo went very still, allowing her to take in the faultless cut of the dark business suit he wore teamed with a bland white shirt and blue silk tie. His brows drew together in a frown. 'Which house?'

'The Lodge…he signed it over to me years ago to ensure that we would always have a home.' Belle's voice faltered slightly because he seemed so taken aback by the news, yet surely he should've known that already as the executor of the estate. 'But bearing in mind the running costs and the children's current needs I'll probably be selling it now.'

'Excuse me for a moment,' Cristo urged, striding out of the room into the one next door and pulling out his phone to call his father's lawyer, Robert Ludlow. If she owned part of the property, he should've been informed of the fact.

Robert's initial disconcertion over Cristo's query trailed away as he trawled through Gaetano's files and then emerged with the facts of a minor legal agreement drawn up about fifteen years earlier, which Robert's elder brother had apparently handled shortly before his retirement. Robert was volubly apologetic for the oversight. Brought up to date, Cristo was triumphantly aware that he knew something Mary Brophy did not appear to know. Under no circumstances would she be selling the Lodge.

Conscious that Cristo Ravelli clearly had not known about the ownership of the Lodge, Belle paced and wondered anxiously why he had not been aware of the fact. She was trying not to recall the fact that the solicitor who had dealt with her mother's estate had found no paperwork confirming the older woman's ownership. He had brushed off the matter and said he would look into it, and at the time Belle had had so many other things on her plate that she hadn't pursued it.

Cristo strolled back into the drawing room with the lithe, unconscious grace of a male who was confident that he was in the strongest position. 'I'm afraid you don't own the Lodge,' he spelt out softly, his Italian accent edging his vowel sounds.

'That's not possible,' Belle countered, her chin rising in challenge. 'Your father told me it was mine—'

'But for your lifetime only, after which it reverts back to the Mayhill estate,' Cristo qualified smoothly.

Suddenly Belle felt as if the ground below her feet had opened to swallow her up. 'That's not what Gaetano led me to believe.'

'My father had a way with words and may have wished you to believe that you *owned* the Lodge but, in fact, you only have the *use* of it.'

A shot of rage flamed through Belle like a lightning strike. That hateful, manipulative man whom her wretched mother had loved! How could he have misled her like that over something so important? Hot colour sprang into her cheeks as she parted her dry lips. 'And this right to live there while…er I am alive, does it devolve to the children after my…er death?' she prompted sickly.

'I'm afraid not.' Cristo Ravelli gave her a specious smile of sympathy, which wouldn't have fooled her in any mood, least of all the one she was in. 'But to all intents and purposes, the Lodge does belong to you for the present. You can't, of course, sell it, use it as security for a loan or indeed make any extensive alterations to it, but you do have the right to live there for as long as you wish.'

Belle had lost every scrap of her angry colour by the time he had finished speaking. It was appalling news, the very worst she could have heard. Her mother was dead and the right to live in the Lodge had died with her, which meant that Belle and her siblings were illegally occupying the house. Indeed, her pretence that she was her mother could be seen by some people as an attempt to defraud. She had taken their ability to live at the Lodge for granted, she registered, stricken. Now she was being punished for it because, in reality, they were about to be made homeless.

'My father was very…astute with regard to money and property,' Cristo murmured softly, watching her standing there, white with shock below the garish make-up, eyes wide and stunned by what he had revealed. 'But I'm willing to find you another property and put it into your name.'

With difficulty, Belle struggled to concentrate. 'And why would you be willing to do that?'

'It will be easier to sell this estate without what would be…in effect…a sitting tenant in the Lodge,' Cristo admitted.

'That…' Belle made a valiant attempt to swallow the massive surge of fury heating her to boiling point and utterly failed to hold it in. 'That…bastard! How could he do that to his own children?' she gasped.

'My father wasn't a sentimental man,' Cristo said drily. 'And he has left a mess in his wake. I have a proposition to put to you which *could* solve all your problems…'

Belle was rigid, furious that she had cursed Gaetano to Cristo's face but unable to overcome the bitter resentment threatening to consume her like a living flame. He was so calm, so assured, so very much in control that she hated him with every fibre in her straining body.

Cristo watched her snatch in another audible breath, eyes green as emeralds in sunlight and literally alight with fury. She was highly volatile, a woman with strong emotions she couldn't hide and everything he had always avoided in her sex. But she looked magnificent and the seductive shimmy of her lush rounded breasts below the silky blouse every time she moved was incredibly attention-grabbing.

'Pro-proposition?' Belle framed shakily, fighting like mad to maintain control over her temper. So, she'd had bad news and she was going to have to deal with it. She stared stonily back at Cristo, clashing with stunning dark eyes nailed to her with unsettling intensity. In the rushing silence that had fallen, her throat closed over and her mouth ran dry.

'I want to ask you to consider the idea of having your children adopted,' Cristo suggested quietly. 'It would surely be best for them to leave their troubled and questionable parentage behind them and have the opportunity to live a normal life.'

'I can't believe you just said that to my face,' Belle confided between gritted teeth of restraint.

'I would make the sacrifice very well worth your while,' Cristo continued evenly as if what he was suggesting were perfectly normal and acceptable. 'My father should have ensured that you have a home and an income but since he hasn't done it, I will take care of it instead.'

'No decent mother would surrender her children for financial gain,' Belle declared in a raw undertone while shooting him a look of scorn that he could even suggest otherwise. 'What sort of women are you used to dealing with?'

'That's not your affair. I am not my father and I have no children,' Cristo replied with cold dignity.

'And don't deserve any either!' Belle lashed back at him. 'For goodness' sake, those children you're talking about are your own brothers and sisters!'

'I do not, and *will* not, acknowledge them as such,' Cristo retorted with icy hauteur.

'Why? Aren't they good enough to be Rav-ellis?' Belle shot back at him resentfully. 'The housekeeper's kids…not very posh, is it? Not quite the right background, am I right? Well, let me tell you something—'

'No. I don't want you to tell me anything while your temper is out of control,' Cristo cut in with the cutting edge of an icy scalpel.

'And you pride yourself on being an iceberg, don't you?' Belle launched back fearlessly, her generous mouth curling with contempt. 'Well, I'm not ashamed to be an emotional person and ready to do what's right no matter how unwel-come or difficult it is!'

'Does your ranting ever get you to the point?' Cristo enquired witheringly.

Belle's slender hands coiled into tight fists. She had never wanted to hit another living per-son before and she was shocked by the fact that she would very much have liked to slap him. How dared he stand there looking down on her and her siblings as if they were so much lesser than him? How dared he suggest that her brothers and sisters be torn away from the people they loved and settled in another home with adoptive parents? Couldn't he appreciate that the children were living, breathing people with emotions and attachments and a desperate need for security after the losses they had already sustained? And couldn't he accept that while Mary Brophy might have had her flaws when it came to picking reliable men, she had also been a wonderful loving mother every day of Belle and her siblings' lives?

'The point is…' Belle breathed in a voice that literally shook with the force of her feelings. 'My mother may only have been a housekeeper and she may have been your father's mistress for years, but she was also a very special, kind and caring person and, having lost her, her children deserve the very best that I can give them.'

'Your…*mother*?' Cristo repeated flatly. 'Mary Brophy was your mother?'

And Belle froze there, her skin slowly turning cold and clammy with shock as she realised what she had revealed in her passionate attempt to bring Cristo round to her point of view. For a moment, she had totally forgotten that she was pretending to be her mother in her desperate need to defend the older woman's memory.

'So, if you're not Mary Brophy...where is she? And who are you?' Cristo framed doggedly, incensed that she had dared to try and fool him.

'I'm Belle Brophy. My mother died about a month after your father. She had a heart attack,' Belle admitted with pained green eyes, accepting that she could no longer continue the pretence and that her own unruly temper had betrayed her when she could least afford for it to do so. Unfortunately Cristo Ravelli's unfeeling detachment and innate air of command and superiority were like vinegar poured on an already raw wound.

'You had no intention of telling me that your mother was dead... You lied to keep the Lodge,' Cristo condemned without hesitation.

Dismay assailed Belle at how quickly he had leapt to that unsavoury conclusion and had assumed she had had a criminal motivation for her masquerade. 'It was nothing to do with the Lodge. Until I came here today I believed my mother owned it and that as her children it became ours after her death,' she reminded him. 'But I didn't think you'd listen to what I want for the children if you knew I was only their sister and not their mother.'

Cristo had a very low tolerance threshold for people who lied to him and tried to deceive him. He was remembering the long-legged redhead crossing the lawn the evening before and guessing that that had been Belle Brophy all along. Outrage swept through his big powerful body, sparking his rarely roused temper. Anger fired his dark eyes gold and he took a sudden livid step towards her. 'You pretended to be your mother... Are you crazy? Or simply downright stupid?'

Her heart suddenly thumping very fast at the dark masculine fury etched in his lean, strong face, Belle sidestepped him and raced for the door. She never hung around long when a man got mad in her vicinity; her childhood had taught her that rage often tumbled over the edge into physical violence.

Cristo closed a hand round her slender forearm as she opened the door. 'You're not going anywhere yet.'

'Let go of my arm!' Belle slung up at him furiously, feeling intimidated by the sheer size of him standing that close. 'I made a mistake but that doesn't give you the right to manhandle me!'

'I'm not manhandling you!' Cristo riposted in disgust. 'But you do owe me an explanation for your peculiar behaviour!'

Her green eyes flared with anger and she yanked her arm violently free of his hold. 'You're a Ravelli! The day I owe you anything there'll be two blue moons in the sky!'

For a split second, Cristo watched her stalk across the hall, stiletto heels tap-tapping, slender spine rigid, red corkscrew curls beginning to untidily descend from her inexpertly arranged chignon. 'Come back here!' he roared at her, out of all patience.

Belle spun round angrily, watching him move towards her, and then she spun out a hand and grabbed up a heavy vase from the table beside her and brandished it like a weapon. 'Don't you dare come any closer!' she warned him.

'Is it normal for you to act like a madwoman?' Cristo asked softly, mastering his fury and his exasperation with the greatest of difficulty.

'I'm going to take you to court, *force* you to recognise the children!' Belle spat back at him in passionate challenge. 'They have legal rights to a share of your father's estate and you can't prevent them from receiving it. And I am not a madwoman.'

An inner chill gripped Cristo at the threat of a court case in which every piece of Gaetano's dirty linen would be aired with the media standing by happy to scoop up and publicise every sordid detail. 'Calm down,' he advised tersely. 'And we'll talk.'

'I don't trust you!' Belle hurled back. 'Let me leave or I'll throw this at you!'

An instant later, Cristo could not comprehend

that he had walked forward in the face of that warning instead of just letting her go, particularly when it was clear that he wouldn't be able to get a sane word out of her until she had calmed down.

Belle flung the vase at him and fled, cringing from the sound of breaking porcelain hitting the tiled floor as she hauled open the front door and raced down the front steps.

'Technically that was an attempt to assault you,' his bodyguard, Rafe, remarked from the stairs as Cristo brushed flakes of porcelain from his suit, his handsome mouth compressed and lean, dark face a grim mask.

'She couldn't hit a barn door at ten paces. Next time, I won't jump out of the way,' Cristo breathed from the steps as he watched her stalk down the driveway, her head held high like an offended queen. She was mad, completely and utterly mad, nutty as a fruitcake. How was he supposed to negotiate with a woman like that? But he *had* to deal with her or face a very public and embarrassing court case.

'There'll *be* a next time?' Rafe could not help responding in surprise.

Cristo's smile was as cold and threatening as a hungry polar bear's. 'Oh, there'll be a next time all right.'

CHAPTER FOUR

'IT'S ALL OUT in the open now, which is much better,' Isa told Belle comfortably. 'Now we all know where we stand.'

Belle dashed a stray curl from her hot brow with a forearm, finished wiping the work surface and dried her hands. She had indulged in an orgy of cleaning since returning to the Lodge. She had needed a physical outlet to work off her excess energy. Her grandmother always reacted to stressful situations with calm and acceptance and when Belle had mentioned worst-case scenarios in the homeless field, Isa had quietly reminded her that it would be a few weeks before Bruno and Donetta returned home for the summer and that that was ample time in which to find somewhere to rent. Belle had had to swallow back the thorny question of how she would *pay* rent because she didn't have the money and Isa didn't either.

Tag began to bark noisily a split second before the doorbell went. Belle walked out to the hall with Tag bouncing excitably at her heels.

Cristo Ravelli stood on the step, six feet four inches tall at the very least and Belle had no heels on, so he towered over her, radiating raw energy and power. His lean, darkly beautiful face was hard and forbidding. 'Miss Brophy?'

'Belle,' she corrected curtly.

Cristo looked his fill from the mane of colourful curls tumbling round her shoulders to the porcelain-pale delicate features that provided the perfect frame for grass-green eyes and a full pink mouth. Out of disguise and bare of the tacky make-up she was absolutely breathtaking.

Belle flushed and parted her lips to ask what he wanted and her grip on the door loosened, allowing Tag to take advantage and dart outside to spring an attack on the visitor.

Cristo got off the step fast as the little dog

snarled and attacked his ankles. Belle squatted down, saying not very effectively, 'No, Tag, no!'

Cristo received the impression that the dog was welcome to eat him alive if he chose to do so.

'Grab Tag!' an older woman snapped from the hall.

Belle gathered the frantic little dog into her arms. 'I'm sorry. He's suspicious of men.'

'Come in, Mr Ravelli,' Isa Kelly invited politely over her granddaughter's crouching figure.

Belle's head came up fast, green eyes stormy. 'I wasn't going to ask—'

'Mr Ravelli is a guest,' her grandmother decreed. 'He will visit and you will talk like civilised people.'

Tag growled at Cristo from the security of Belle's arms. 'Your father kicked him…so did mine,' she confided grudgingly. 'That's why he doesn't like men. He's too old now to change his ways.'

The older woman studied Cristo, hostility

creeping into her voice, despite the civility of her words.

Cristo strolled into a hideous lounge with pink walls, hot-pink sofas and embellished with so many pink frills and ostentatious fake-flower arrangements that it was as if his worst nightmare had come to life. 'I've never liked dogs,' he confided.

A curly-haired toddler clamped both arms round his leg before he could sit down.

'No, Franco,' Belle scolded.

'Or kids,' Cristo added unapologetically.

Franco looked up at him. He had Gaetano's eyes and Cristo found that sight so unnerving that he sat down with the kid still clamped awkwardly to one leg.

'Man,' Franco pronounced with an air of discovery and satisfaction.

'He's a wee bit starved of male attention,' Belle breathed, setting down the dog to grab the toddler in his place and convey him struggling and loudly protesting into the kitchen with her.

'Cristo drinks black coffee,' her grandmother told her from the doorway.

Belle gritted her teeth but she knew that the older woman was talking sense; she *did* have to talk to Cristo and, having set out her expectations, at least he already knew her plans.

Cristo ignored the dog snarling at him from below the coffee table. It was little and grey around the muzzle and should have known better in his opinion than to embark on a battle it couldn't possibly win. Cristo never wasted his time on lost causes or thankless challenges but Belle would, no doubt, have been pleased to learn that her threat had focused his powerful intellect as nothing else could have done.

The instant the tray of coffee and biscuits arrived, Cristo rose back upright, feeling suffocated amidst all that horrible pinkness. 'I don't want you to take the question of the children's parentage into court.'

'Tough,' Belle said succinctly, not one whit perturbed by his statement because she could hardly have expected him to be supportive on that score. 'My brothers and sisters have been ignored and passed over far too many times. I want them to have what they're entitled to.'

'A few years ago, Gaetano sold up most of his assets and he salted away the proceeds in overseas trusts, which no Irish court will be able to access,' Cristo volunteered. 'With the exception of the sale of the Mayhill estate there is very little cash for you to demand a share of on behalf of your siblings.'

'I'm not looking for a fortune for them.'

'I have a better idea,' Cristo told her.

'I imagine that you *always* have a better idea,' Belle quipped helplessly, leaning back against the kitchen door with defensively folded arms while she wondered how any man could look so fit and vital clad in a tailored business suit that belonged in a boardroom.

She was slim as a whip in her tight faded jeans and an off-the-shoulder black tee that revealed an entrancing glimpse of a narrow white shoulder bisected by a black strap that Cristo savoured, glorying in the fact that he was now free to appreciate her glowing beauty while he speculated as to whether or not she was that pale all over, her skin in vibrant contrast to her bright hair and eyes. The instant he developed an erection, he regretted that evocative thought.

'I will make a settlement on your siblings in compensation for their not pursuing their rights through the courts,' Cristo delivered, half turning away from her to look out of the window overlooking the drive.

'We don't want Ravelli charity,' Belle traded, lifting her chin.

'But it wouldn't be charity. As you said, they're my father's children and I should make good on that for all our sakes. My family would find a court case embarrassing,' Cristo admitted tight-mouthed.

Belle didn't shift an inch. 'Why should I care about that?'

'Publicity is a double-edged sword,' Cristo warned her. 'The media loves sleaze. Your mother won't emerge well from the story. At least three of the children were born while Gaetano was still married.'

At that blunt reminder, a veil of colour burned up below Belle's fair complexion. 'That can't be helped and Mum can't be hurt now. I have to consider the children's future. I want them to have the right to use the Ravelli name.'

'No court that I know of has the ability to bestow that right when no marriage took place between the parents,' Cristo countered, exasperated by her pig-headedness. 'You're being unreasonable. If you keep this out of court and allow me to handle things discreetly, I will be generous. It's the best offer you're going to get.'

'Forgive me for my lack of trust. As I learned today with regard to the ownership of this house, your father was a good teacher.'

'I will not allow you to take this sordid mess into a public courtroom,' Cristo spelt out harshly. 'If you do that I will fight you every step of the way and I warn you—you don't want me as an enemy.'

'Fight me all you like…it's still going to

court,' Belle replied thinly. 'We have nothing to lose and everything to gain.'

'What would it take for you to drop this idea?' Cristo growled, almost shuddering at the threat of how much damage a media smear campaign could do to his brother. Zarif's standing in Vashir was delicate, his having only recently ascended the throne. The last thing Zarif needed right now was a great big horrible scandal that would give all too many people the impression that he was from a sleazy family background and was far from being the right ruler for a very conservative country. Zarif, Cristo reminded himself grimly, had already taken the fall for revealing Nik's biggest secret to Nik's estranged wife, Betsy, when the first careless spilling of that secret was entirely Cristo's fault.

'I'd probably be asking for the impossible,' Belle admitted ruefully, 'but I want my siblings to have the lifestyle they would have enjoyed had Gaetano married my mother. It's very unfair that they should have to pay the price for the fact that he didn't marry her.'

'You're being irrational,' Cristo condemned, impatiently, moving out of the room. 'You can't change the past.'

'I don't want to change the past. I simply want to right the wrongs that have been done to my siblings.'

'Leave the past behind you and move on.'

'Easy for you to say,' Belle quipped. 'Not so easy in practice. And I'm not irrational—'

In the hall, Cristo swung round, surprisingly light on his feet for so large and powerfully built a man. 'You're the most irrational woman I've ever met.'

Belle collided with his stunning dark eyes and for a timeless moment the world stopped turning and she stopped breathing.

'And for some reason I find it incredibly sexy,' Cristo purred the admission, his accent roughening his dark deep drawl as he flicked her tee shirt back up over her exposed shoulder with a long careless forefinger.

'You can't get round me. I'm not as naïve as my mother was,' Belle told him tartly.

'Wake up and smell the roses, *cara*. You're a child trying to play with the grown-ups,' Cristo told her thickly, his intimate intonation vibrating down her taut spinal cord.

Suddenly, Belle was short of breath and she stared up at him, her eyes very wide and scornful. 'A child? Is that the best you can do on the insult front?'

'I wasn't trying to insult you.' Up that close his dark eyes had tiny gold flecks like stars. His hand curved to her shoulder and the scent of clean, warm male overlaid with a faint hint of cologne ignited a burst of heat low in Belle's tummy. Just as suddenly she was locked into his eyes and it was as though her feet were encased in concrete and she literally *couldn't* move. He lowered his handsome dark head and took her parted lips with a scorching urgency that sent something frighteningly wild and alive flying through her like an explosive charge. It was a fiery kiss and like no other she had experienced. The minute his tongue plunged into the tender interior of her mouth, it sent a wave of violent response crashing through her, and she was lost. Her hands roamed from his broad shoulders up into his luxuriant dark hair while she rejoiced in the taste of him, the unique sexual flavour of a dominant and surprisingly passionate male. His arms tightened round her, long fingers smoothing down her spine to pin her into un-compromising awareness of his erection. She gasped beneath the thrust of his tongue, mind flying free to picture a much more sexual join-ing and craving that completion with a strength that started an ache between her thighs.

The sheer intensity of what she was feeling totally spooked Belle. With a startled sound of rejection, she pushed him back from her. 'No, we're not doing this!' she told him furiously.

Dark eyes veiled, Cristo stepped back and drew in a long, deep, steadying breath. *Maled-izione!* He was too aroused to be comfortable with the sensation or the woman who had got him into that condition. 'I seem to recall that I was trying to persuade you not to take private family business into a court of law,' he murmured flatly.

Belle shot him a disconcerted glance, unable to credit that he could act as frozen as ever in the wake of that passionate kiss. Passion, it seemed, didn't control Cristo Ravelli. All in the space of a moment she resented his assurance, was insulted by his cool indifference and furious that she hadn't fought him off. But, my goodness, he could kiss. That mortifying thought crept through her mind no matter how hard she tried to kill it dead.

Belle had done a lot of kissing and not much else as a student, very much hoping to experience a volcanic reaction that would signal that all-important spark of true, overwhelming physical attraction. Now fate was having the last laugh by finally serving up that long-awaited, miraculously special kiss and it was happening with the *wrong* man. She had no doubt that Cristo Ravelli was wrong in every way for her. He was stuffy and cold and unfeeling and she was a warm, emotional and impulsive individual.

'I'm sorry. I'm going to do what's best for my siblings and take this matter to court to get it sorted out,' Belle told him curtly.

'You can't,' Cristo countered with chilling bite. 'It will damage other people. You and your siblings are not the only individuals likely to be affected by this.'

'I don't care about anyone else,' Belle admitted truthfully. 'I want my brothers and sisters to be able to hold their heads high and know who they are without shame.'

'You want the impossible,' Cristo derided, turning on his heel.

'No, I want justice.'

Justice! Cristo reflected contemptuously, a deep sense of frustration ruling him, for Cristo never backed down and never failed to find solutions to problems. Damage limitation was his speciality. How could it be justice that Zarif's throne would be rocked by the extent of Gaetano's infidelity and the revelation of his secret family in Ireland? Like father, like son, Zarif's critics would sneer. Mary Brophy had made her choices when she chose to get involved with a married man and have his children. Her daughter, Belle, had too much pride and her resentment of the Ravelli family, or, more specifically, his father, had persuaded her that she could somehow rewrite history. But washing the family dirty linen in public was *not* going to make those children feel that they could raise their heads high. No, it was much more likely to shame them by depicting their parents in ways they would never forget. No child of Gaetano's had *ever* been proud of him or his name. Gaetano had been a cruelly selfish and uninterested parent.

Ironically, Cristo had always believed growing up that he would be a better man than his father and now he wondered what had happened to that dream and at what point cynicism had killed that honourable goal stone dead. He knew that he had not once considered the plight of Mary Brophy's children from any viewpoint other than his own. He was a pragmatic man and he knew he was selfish. But even *he* recognised that Belle Brophy was too young and her grandmother too old to take on full responsibility for Gaetano's children. Cristo was suddenly very conscious that those kids, right down to the little one with his father's eyes, were his flesh and blood too, even though he didn't want to recognise that unwelcome fact.

And then the answer to the problem came to him in a sudden shocking moment of truth. He recoiled from the prospect at first, but as he filtered through the list of challenges he currently faced and that solution ticked every box he began to mull it over as a genuine possibility. It was not as though he were ever likely to fall in love again. Indeed it was a wonder it had happened even once to a male as detached from emotion as he was, he reasoned grimly. Gaetano and Mary's affair could be decently buried and the children's antecedents concealed from the media. As for Belle, in the role he envisaged, which was frankly Belle reclining wearing only a winsome smile on his bed in London, well, she would be perfect there, he reflected with the very first flicker of enthusiasm for the challenge of sacrificing his freedom for the greater good.

Belle suffered a restless night of sleep. She relived the kiss again and again and got hot and bothered while tossing and turning in guilty discomfiture. Cristo was a Ravelli just like Gaetano and the very last man alive she should enjoy kissing. In the morning, she made breakfast for the children on automatic pilot because her brain felt fuzzy and slow. There had been too much agonising over whether or not going to court was the right thing to do for the children, she decided irritably. She did not have a choice. There had never been a choice and there was no way on earth that she planned to trust in any promises made by Cristo Ravelli, who would undoubtedly be every bit as slippery in such delicate negotiations as his late father had proved to be. Exasperated by the constant parade of anxious thoughts weighing her down,

Belle saw the twins off to school and then told her grandmother that she was taking Franco down to the beach.

When he reached the beach, Cristo had the pleasure of seeing Belle looking relaxed for the first time. Her wild mane of curls was blowing back from her face in the breeze that plastered her jeans and her blue tee to her lithe, shapely body. She was engaged in throwing a stone into the sea while the leg-clinging toddler bounced up and down in excitement and the dog circled them both barking noisily. Espying Cristo first, the Jack Russell raced across the sand to attack.

'No!' Cristo thundered as he strode across the sand.

Tag cringed and rolled over and stuck his four little legs up in the air, beady eyes telegraphing terror.

'You didn't need to shout at him,' Belle criticised, rushing over to crouch down and pet the little animal. 'Look how frightened he is! He's very sensitive.'

'I'm a little sensitive to being bitten,' Cristo murmured drily.

'Man!' the toddler exclaimed and immediately went for Cristo's left leg. Cristo froze, wondering if he could *do* it—actually take on the whole bunch of them and survive with his dignity and sanity intact. He wasn't a family man, he hadn't a clue how a normal family functioned and didn't really want to find out.

Belle was looking up at him, her lovely face flushed and self-conscious, clear green eyes wide above her dainty freckled nose, and her vibrant beauty in that instant scoured his mind clean of all such thoughts. She made him think about sex, lots and lots and lots of sex, and on one level that unnerved him and on another it turned him so hard it literally hurt.

Belle stood up. Tag, the terrified dog, was clasped to her bosom, and now giving Cristo a rather smug look. 'Did Isa tell you where I was?'

'I could be down here for a walk.'

Belle raised a fine auburn brow, scanning

his lean, powerful body with assessing eyes. It amazed her that a man who spent so much time in a business suit could be so well built but there he was: broad of shoulder and chest, lean of hip and long of leg with not even the hint of jowls or a paunch. Clearly, he kept fit. And although she had long thought business suits were boring Cristo's dark, perfectly tailored designer suit screamed class and sophistication and was cut close to his powerful thighs and lean hips, directing her attention to areas she didn't normally appraise on men. Her colour heightening, she tore her attention from the prominent bulge at his crotch and dropped it down to his highly polished shoes, which were caked with sand, and she wondered why he couldn't just admit that he had come looking for her.

'You didn't come down here for a walk dressed like that.'

'Sand brushes off,' he fielded carelessly as she settled the dog down on the beach and he scampered off.

In silence, Belle studied Cristo's lean, extravagantly handsome features, heat blossoming in her pelvis and butterflies flying free in her tummy. She felt as clumsy and ill at ease as a schoolgirl in the presence of her idol. But then was it any wonder that she was embarrassed? She had looked at his body and positively delighted in the strikingly strong muscular definition inherent in his build. She could not recall ever doing that to a man before. But the need to look at Cristo felt as necessary as the need to breathe. In reaction to that humiliating truth she flushed to the roots of her hair, mortified by her failure to control her reaction to his looks and dark, charismatic appeal.

Cristo reached down to detach the toddler's painful grip from his leg. *Starved of male attention*, he recalled, thinking that he could certainly understand that. Neither in childhood nor adulthood had Gaetano ever touched him or, indeed, enquired after his well-being. 'We have to talk,' he said succinctly.

'There's nothing more to talk about. We said it all last night,' Belle tossed over a slim shoulder as she started down the beach again and extended her hand. 'Franco, come here!'

'No!' the toddler said stubbornly and, deprived of Cristo's leg, grasped a handful of his trousers instead, making it difficult for Cristo to walk.

Cristo expelled his breath in a slow measured hiss. 'I placed the Mayhill estate on the market this morning,' he fired at her rudely turned back.

Belle came to a dead halt, her narrow spine suddenly rigid as panic leapt inside her at the prospect of losing the roof over their heads. There was certainly no room for them all to squeeze into Isa's one-bedroom apartment in the village. She stared out to sea but the soothing sound of the surf washing the sand smooth failed to work its usual magic. She turned her bright head, green eyes glittering. 'Couldn't that have waited for a few weeks?'

Cristo took his time crossing the sand to join her, her little brother clinging to whatever part of Cristo he could reach and finally stretching up to grip the corner of his suit jacket with sandy fingers. 'No. I want the property sold as soon as possible. I want Gaetano's life here to remain a secret.'

'And what about us? Where are we supposed to go?' Belle demanded heatedly, her temper rising. 'It takes time to relocate.'

'You'll have at least a month to find somewhere else,' Cristo fielded without perceptible sympathy while he watched the breeze push the soft, clinging cotton of her top against her breasts, defining the full rounded swells and her pointed nipples. The heavy pulse at his groin went crazy and he clenched his teeth together, willing back his arousal.

'That's not very long. Bruno and Donetta will be home from school for the summer soon. Five children take up a lot of space… They're your brothers and sisters too, so you should *care* about what happens to them!' Belle launched back at him in furious condemnation.

'Which is why I'm here to suggest that we get married and *make* a home for them together,'

Cristo countered with harsh emphasis as he wondered for possibly the very first time in his life whether he really did know what he was doing.

'*Married?*' Belle repeated aghast, wondering if she'd missed a line or two in the conversation. 'What on earth are you talking about?'

'You said that you wanted your siblings to enjoy the Ravelli name and lifestyle. I can only make that happen by marrying you and adopting them.'

Frowning in confusion, Belle fell back a step, in too much shock to immediately respond. 'Is this a joke?' she asked when she had finally found her voice again.

'Why would I joke about something so serious?'

Belle shrugged. 'How would I know? You thought it was acceptable to suggest to their mother that she give them up to be adopted,' she reminded him helplessly.

'I'm not joking,' Cristo replied levelly, a stray

shard of sunlight breaking through the clouds to slant across his lean, strong face.

All over again, Belle studied him in wonder because he had the smouldering dark beauty of a fallen angel. His brilliant dark eyes were nothing short of stunning below the thick screen of his lashes and suddenly she felt as breathless as though someone were standing on her lungs.

'I'm a practical man and I'm suggesting a practical marriage which would fulfil *all* our needs,' Cristo continued smoothly. 'You're aware that I don't want a court case. I also want to prevent the squalid story of Gaetano and his housekeeper leaking into the public domain. You would have to agree not to discuss the children's parentage with anyone but nobody need tell any lies either. As far as anyone need know, the children are simply your orphaned brothers and sisters.'

Belle breathed in deep and slow but it still didn't clear her head. 'I can't believe you're suggesting this.'

'You didn't give me a choice, did you? The

threat of a court case piled on the pressure. *Are you prepared to settle this out of court?'* Cristo studied her enquiringly.

Belle didn't hesitate. 'No.'

Cristo raised a sleek ebony brow. 'Then what's your answer?'

'It's not that simple,' Belle protested.

'Isn't it? I'm offering you everything you said you wanted.'

Her lashes flickered above her strained eyes. She felt cornered and trapped. 'Well, yes, but… *marriage*? I could hardly be expecting that development!'

Annoyance lanced through Cristo. It was his very first proposal of marriage and he had never before even considered proposing to a woman. Without a shade of vanity he knew he was rich, good-looking and very eligible and yet she was hesitating and he was grimly amused by his irritation.

'Look, I'll think it over until tonight,' Belle muttered uncomfortably.

'*Di niente*…no problem,' Cristo fielded, his

wide, sensual mouth compressed. 'By the way…I mean a *real* marriage.'

'Real…?' Belle spluttered to a halt, the tip of her tongue stealing out to wet her dry lower lip. His intent dark gaze flashed pure naked gold to that tiny movement. Heated colour swept her face as she grasped his meaning in growing disbelief. 'You'd expect me to *sleep* with you?'

'Of course,' Cristo murmured with an indolent assurance that suggested that that idea was entirely normal and acceptable. 'I have no plans to emulate my father and entertain mistresses while I'm married. And I don't want a wife who plays around behind my back either. That kind of lifestyle would not provide a stable home for the children.'

Belle got his point, she really did, but she flushed scarlet at the thought of sharing a bed with him, suddenly very conscious of her own lack of sexual experience. Growing up, she'd had to combat the expectations of the local boys who saw her mother as free and easy in that department and she had had to prove over and over again that she was different. Saying no had been a matter of pride and self-preservation, but as she got older that conditioning along with other needs and insecurities had influenced her and *trusting* a man enough to drop her guard and make love had proved to be even more of a challenge for Belle.

Cristo settled a business card into her limp hand and she stared down at it blankly.

'My private cell number. Let me know by seven this evening, *bellezza mia*,' he instructed with unblemished cool. 'That way I can make an immediate start on the arrangements.'

CHAPTER FIVE

'*DON'T DO THIS...don't do this...*' Isa's constant refrain was still sounding like a death knell in Belle's ears as she climbed out of the car Cristo had sent to collect her and mounted the steps that led up into the chapel of St Jude's. She was wearing an elegant but rather plain vintage dress with a boat-shaped lace neckline. It was her late mother's wedding gown.

The symbolism of that gesture had appealed to her and in the three weeks that had passed since she last saw Cristo she'd had the dress lengthened to suit her greater height. Mary might never have got her Ravelli to the altar but her daughter was succeeding where she had failed, Belle could not help reflecting with guilty satisfaction. She knew it wasn't right to feel that way because Cristo was not Gaetano and he had not committed his father's sins but she couldn't help it. She was the talk of the neighbourhood, for nobody was quite sure how she had hooked a husband who had only set foot in Ireland for the first time less than a month ago. Indeed there was a crowd of well-wishers waiting outside the old church, quietly ignoring Cristo's request that the wedding be regarded as a private affair.

Of course, Cristo definitely knew how to garner support and respect in the locals, Belle conceded ruefully. He had decided not to sell Mayhill but to instead gift the historic house to the village as a community centre and endow it for the future. Money talked, money certainly talked *very* loudly in an area where incomes were low and jobs were few. Mayhill would put the village on the map by becoming a tourist attraction and its maintenance and the business prospects it would provide would offer many employment opportunities. And naturally, it was tacitly and silently understood by the recipients of Cristo's extraordinary largesse that his father's affair with Mary Brophy and the birth of their children were matters to be buried in the darkest, deepest closet never to see the light of day again.

Her sisters, thirteen-year-old Donetta and eight-year-old Lucia, were beaming at her from a front pew. Her brothers Bruno, Pietro and little Franco were beside them. Bruno was frowning, too intelligent to be fooled by the surface show and still suspicious of what was happening to his family.

'Do you really *want* to marry Gaetano's son?' Bruno had demanded the night before when he had returned from school with Donetta, both teenagers granted special leave for the occasion of their sister's wedding.

'It was love at first sight,' Belle had lied, determined to remove the lines of concern from his brow and the too anxious look from his sensitive gaze. 'And how can you ask me that?'

'I'm not saying I don't believe you…but it seems very convenient in the circumstances. I mean, here we are, broke, virtually homeless and sinking fast and along comes Cristo Ravelli *in* the rescue boat and suddenly our every dream is coming true,' Bruno had recited thinly. 'It doesn't *feel* real to me—it's too good to be true. How did you finally bury the hatchet?'

'What hatchet?'

'You grew up hating the Ravelli family and now all of a sudden you're *marrying* one of them?'

'He's your brother,' Belle had reminded the teenager stubbornly.

'He's a super-rich banker and as sharp as a whip. It's you I'm concerned about. What do you know about being married to a guy like that?' Bruno had asked worriedly. 'He lives in a different world.'

But right now, Cristo was in Belle's world, she savoured helplessly, finally allowing herself to look at the tall, well-built male waiting for her at the altar. Not an iota of the traditional bridegroom's nervous tension showed on his lean, darkly handsome features. In fact he might just have been an attendant at someone else's wedding for all the awareness he was showing.

Unconsciously, Belle's chin lifted as if she had been challenged; her heart was pounding fast as a hammer blow behind her ribs and her spine was rigid with all the tension he lacked. After all, she had barely slept since texting him a single word, 'Yes', on the day he had proposed to her on the beach.

Accepting had taken a massive amount of courage and she had garnered that courage only by focusing on the advantages of marrying Cristo Ravelli and suppressing all awareness of the downsides. Her family would finally be safe, absolutely *safe and secure* and that was the bottom line and the only important thing she should concentrate on. What it cost her personally wasn't important and couldn't be weighed on the scale of such things.

After all, she had never been in love and was even more certain that she didn't want to fall in love with anyone. Her memories of her mother's unhappiness during Gaetano's long absences were still fresh as a daisy. Mary had only really come alive when Gaetano was around. Every time he departed it had broken Mary's heart afresh and he would leave her pining and life-less with only the occasional brief phone call to anticipate while she counted the weeks and days until his next visit. Belle had kept one of those painstakingly numbered calendars as a reminder of what such unstinting, unhesitating love, loyalty and devotion could do to wreck a woman's life. Mary had *lived* for Gaetano. Belle only wanted to live for her family and ensure that they enjoyed a much happier and more sta-ble childhood than she had received.

Isa was staying on in the Lodge for the sum-mer and had insisted that Bruno, Donetta and the twins stay on there with her, leaving only Franco to stay with Belle because her little brother was too attached to her to be separated from her for weeks on end. 'You get your mar-riage sorted out before you uproot the kids to London and new schools and all the rest of it,' her grandmother had told her bluntly. 'You know I don't approve of what you're doing and if there's a risk that this marriage will only last as long as it takes you to come to your senses, you shouldn't drag the children into it with you.'

Belle had argued until she was finally forced to acknowledge that the older woman was talking good sense. Of course there was a chance that she and Cristo wouldn't make a go of their 'practical' marriage. She would have to make a success of their relationship before she could risk disrupting the children's lives and bringing them to London to live on a permanent basis. That was a pretty tall order when she had, more or less, agreed to marry a complete stranger.

Thinking along those lines, Belle decided she had to have been insane to say yes with so little thought. It was not that she had not thought about things, simply that she had avoided considering the negative aspects. Going to bed with Cristo had to be one of the more intimidating negative aspects, she conceded, turning hot and cold at the very thought of it, but just *living* with Cristo, indeed with *any* man, would surely be the ultimate challenge.

Wintry dark eyes slashed with gold by the

sunlight piercing the stained-glass window behind him, Cristo watched his bride approach. She looked absolutely amazing in white, red gold curls tumbling round her narrow shoulders, her bright head crowned by a simple seed-pearl coronet. Lust engulfed Cristo in a drowning wave and his wide, sensual mouth compressed hard. *Maledizione!* He was convinced that he had never wanted a woman as much before yet he was equally convinced that she would ultimately prove as disappointing as her predecessors. Of course she would, he reflected impatiently, being no fan of optimism or fairy stories. But at least he already knew the worst of her, which was that she was a virtual black-mailer, a gold-digger and a social climber. Better the devil you know than the one you don't, he conceded sardonically and he was exceptionally well versed on the habits and needs of mercenary women.

Her hand trembled in his when he slid on the wedding ring. A nice touch, he thought cynically, a bridal display of nerves and modesty and utterly wasted on Cristo, who was the last man alive likely to be impressed or taken in by such pretences. He was gaining a very beautiful and desirable wife, he reminded himself doggedly, and putting a lid on the threat of an unsavoury scandal. Even his brothers didn't know what he was doing, for the last thing he would have risked was bringing either of them to the scene of Gaetano's reckless shenanigans in this little Irish village.

Cristo pretty much ignored Belle on the short drive back to the Lodge, where a small catered buffet and drinks had been laid on for the family and the few friends invited. It had not escaped Belle's notice that Cristo had not invited a single person and it bothered her, making her wonder if he was ashamed of her and her humble background and lack of designer polish.

Bruno walked up to Cristo in the hall. 'Could we have a word?' he asked, youthful face taut and pale.

Bruno was the living image of Zarif as a teenager and that likeness had unsettled Cristo at their first brief and awkward meeting the evening before. It seemed that Gaetano had stamped the Ravelli genes very firmly on all his offspring.

'Is there a problem?' Cristo enquired, a fine ebony brow lifting.

The teenager backed into the small space at the foot of the stairs and said gruffly, 'If you hurt my sister like your father hurt my mother, I swear I'll kill you.'

Cristo almost laughed but a stray shard of compassion squashed his amusement when he recalled his own turbulent teenaged years. In any case the warning had all the hallmarks of a prepared speech and, having delivered it, Bruno was backing off fast, troubled brown eyes nervously pinned to Cristo as though he was expecting an immediate physical attack. Before the boy could leave, Christo called him back.

'We're family now and I'm not like my father in any way,' Cristo responded very quietly to the teenager. 'I have no desire to hurt any woman.'

From a tactful distance, Belle absorbed that little interplay. Although she hadn't heard the conversation, she suspected that Bruno had probably been very rude in his outspoken need to protect her and she recognised with a sense of unfamiliar warmth that Cristo had handled her kid brother with surprising sympathy. *Their* kid brother, she mentally corrected, yet there it was—Cristo might not be ready yet to acknowledge that blood tie, but he had restrained both his cutting tongue and his temper when he dealt with Bruno and she was grateful for his kindness.

As Bruno moved hurriedly away, his goal evidently accomplished, Cristo studied the slim dark man whose eyes were welded to Belle's vibrant face as she talked to her grandmother's friends. Cristo stiffened, aggression powering through him as he recognised the son of the land agent, Petrie. Petrie's son, Mark, was attracted to his wife. *His* wife. The shock of that designation ricocheted through Cristo as well and he suppressed his awareness of both strange reactions. He concentrated on Belle instead and watched when she fell still the instant she saw him looking at her, enabling him to clearly see her sudden tension and insecurity.

The golden power of Cristo's gaze was almost mesmeric in its intensity and Belle gulped down the rest of the wine in her glass.

'Eat something,' Isa instructed. 'You didn't have any breakfast.'

Belle accepted the sandwich extended for the sake of peace, for although her tummy felt hollow it had nothing to do with hunger. 'I'll go and get changed,' she said uneasily, ruffling Franco's curly head where he stood by her side.

Cristo was still in the hall, detached from the small crowd by a barrier of reserve that chilled her.

'He's not very friendly, is he?' her sister Donetta whispered in her ear.

Belle forced a smile, cursing Cristo's detachment and his clear reluctance to use the opportunity to get to know his younger siblings. 'He's just shy.'

'Shy?' Donetta gasped in surprise.

'*Very* shy,' Belle lied, wanting to lay the teenager's concerns to rest. 'It'll be different when he gets to know all of you properly.'

And the burden of ensuring that it would be different was on *her* shoulders, Belle acknowledged apprehensively, registering what a challenge she had set herself. Cristo had been raised an only child and a family the size of hers had to be a shock to his reticent nature. Franco was tugging at his jacket, looking up at Cristo with adoring brown eyes, and Cristo was at least tolerating the child, she reasoned ruefully, wondering if that was the most she could hope for from him when it came to the children. And her? Would he only be *tolerating* her as well? A shiver of distaste at that image ran down her back until she was warmed by the recollection of his considered response to Bruno.

'Where are you going?' Cristo enquired when she brushed past him to head for the stairs.

'I'm getting changed…for the flight you mentioned,' she extended awkwardly, lashes screening her strained green eyes.

He was her husband, for goodness' sake, and he had decreed that they would be flying out of Ireland within hours of the ceremony. She had thought about arguing but then had seen no point in trying to put off the inevitable. She had given up her life to enter his and leaving home was the first step in that process.

'No. I like the dress. Don't take it off.'

Thoroughly taken aback by the command, Belle glanced up at him in astonishment at the request. 'I can't trudge through an airport dressed like this.'

'I have a private jet and we won't be trudging anywhere. Don't take the dress off, *bellezza mia,*' Cristo instructed sibilantly, a strong dark forefinger curling below her chin to lift it so that she collided with smouldering golden eyes. '*I* want to be the one who takes it off.'

Face burning, breath coming in tortured bursts, Belle fled upstairs, barely able to credit that he had said that to her. She had read about male fantasies and he had just told her his with a lack of embarrassment that made her all the more conscious of her own ignorance. He was already fantasising about removing her bridal gown. It was a useful message as to what went on in Cristo's arrogant head. While she was worrying about him getting to know and like their brothers and sisters *he* was thinking about sex. Was that all their marriage meant to him? Sex and the threat of a big scandal removed?

And if it was, what on earth could she do about it? All her gran's warnings and dire predictions came crashing down on her at once. What if he was cruel? Unfaithful? Belle swallowed hard, mastering her tumultuous emotions. You made your bed, now you have to lie on it…*literally*, she told herself sternly as she checked that she had packed the most essential things for herself and Franco.

Franco cried and begged to get out of his car seat all the way to the airport. Aware of the irritation Cristo couldn't hide and with her own

spirits low at having left home and everything
and almost everyone familiar behind her for
goodness knew how long, Belle tried to dis-
tract the child.

'Why did your mother have so many children
with my father?' Cristo asked suddenly.

'She always wanted a big family and I think
the kids were her compensation for not seeing
much of your father,' Belle opined and then,
hesitating, added, 'Gaetano wanted nothing to
do with them though. When he was here they
went to stay with Isa and maybe only saw him
once for about ten minutes and it would be very
strained. He just wasn't interested.'

'He was the same with me and my brothers.'

'I *hated* him!' Belle admitted in a driven undertone. 'I felt guilty about that when he was
killed in the crash.'

'You shouldn't, *cara*,' Cristo parried. 'He was
a very selfish man, who lived only for his pleasure and his profit. Nothing else mattered to
him.'

Belle settled into her seat on Cristo's opulent

private jet. Franco was in the sleeping compartment and, once she had settled her little brother down for his nap, Cristo had informed her that he had hired a nanny for the child, who would be waiting when they reached their destination.

'Which...*is*?'

'Italy. I'm taking you to my home in Italy.'

'Venice...we're going to Venice?' Belle carolled in sudden excitement.

'No, that is where my mother and stepfather live. I inherited a house in Umbria, which has belonged to my mother's family for generations. Sorry, it's not Venice,' Cristo quipped.

'Won't your mother be upset that she wasn't at your wedding?' Belle prompted, shooting him a look of wide-eyed curiosity.

'I doubt it. Anything that reminds Giulia of Gaetano puts her in a very bad mood,' Cristo admitted, compressing his lips. 'She never recovered from what he put her through. You couldn't be in her company for five minutes before she told you that he stole the best years

of her life, robbed her blind and slept with—
among others—her best friend and her maid.'

'Good grief...' Belle breathed, reeling from
that blunt admission.

During the flight, even with his laptop open
in front of him, Cristo found his attention con-
tinually straying from the financial report he
was checking. He studied Belle's delicate profile from below his dense lashes, marvelling at
the display of innocence and vulnerability that
she continued to exude. Was he supposed to
be impressed? Did he strike her as that stupid?
After all, Mary Brophy's daughter was considerably shrewder than her mother had ever been
because she had not hesitated to use Gaetano's
children as a weapon to enrich herself. But his
awareness of that aspect of her less than stellar
character faded whenever Cristo looked at her,
appreciating the vibrancy of her Titian curls
against her porcelain-pale skin, the clarity of
her beautiful green eyes, the feminine elegance
of the fingers and unpainted nails adorning the
slim hands that held a magazine. She always

looked so amazingly natural, he registered, black brows drawing together in a bemused frown as he questioned the depth of his fascination and hurriedly returned to his financial report, trying and singularly failing to rustle up an immediate image of Betsy's face.

The nanny, Teresa, a middle-aged woman with a warm smile, greeted them at the airport and gathered up Franco with enough appreciation to persuade Belle that her little brother would enjoy the best of attention. Though quite what Cristo expected her to do with her time while someone else looked after Franco, she had no idea. After driving through miles of extensively cultivated agricultural land the sun was going down fast when the limousine began to climb mountain roads with hairpin bends that soon slowed the speed of their passage.

'It feels as if we're travelling to the end of the world,' Belle commented.

'As far as my mother was concerned, the Palazzo Maddalena, named for one of her ancestors, might as well have been. It was never her style.'

And as the car travelled slowly towards to the massive stone building presiding over the hill tops, Belle knew it wasn't her style either and her heart and her courage sank to their lowest ever level. For the first time it really hit her exactly what marrying Cristo entailed and the little girl whose earliest home had been a tiny house was ready to surface again because the adult woman was overpowered by the sheer size and grandeur of the property confronting her. Ancient mellowed stone encased the three-storeys-tall palazzo, which had graceful wings spreading to either side. Elaborate terraced gardens in an ornamental pattern spread down the hill in front of it and behind the solid bulk of the building loomed the imposing snow-capped tops of the Sibillini mountain range.

As pale as a newly created ghost, Belle climbed out of the car, her lovely face frozen and expressionless, her wedding gown glimmering eerily in the twilight. Cristo surveyed her with a level of satisfaction that disconcerted him. *His* wife, *his* home where he was free to be himself. *Her* tension, though, was not a surprise because Cristo was convinced he knew precisely why Belle would have preferred Venice. What was the point of marrying a billionaire if she couldn't enjoy the expected rich advantages that came with the wedding ring? In Venice she could have partied with his mother's wealthy and famous friends and shopped in expensive boutiques and jewellery stores. An ancestral palazzo in the mountains was no fair exchange.

'It's a great place for a honeymoon,' Cristo informed her with something that just might have been amusement glimmering in his keen gaze.

A honeymoon? Well, she *was* married. But why was he laughing at her? Did he also see the ludicrous gulf between a boy raised in a gilded Venetian palace and the housekeeper's daughter? How could he fail to? A tide of self-conscious colour washed Belle's complexion as they entered the enormous palazzo. She knew time was running out. They had dined on the plane, so not even the need to eat could be stretched out to lengthen the evening ahead. For good-

ness' sake, she urged herself, lighten up, *wise*
up. This was the deal; this was the agreement
that would ensure her siblings received everything that should have been theirs from birth.
They would grow up secure and safe as Ravel-
lis and nobody would have an excuse to mock
them or sneer at them. They would have the
best of educations and opportunities to equip
them to enter adult life. They would never have
to worry about where their next meal was coming from. As she listed the countless benefits of
having married Cristo Ravelli, Belle's breathing slowly steadied and she steeled her spine.

Franco clutched at her dress as they mounted
the stairs and the manservant who had let them
in showed them first to a nursery suite where
the nanny tried to detach Franco from Belle.
But Franco didn't like strange places and he
started to sob and clutch at his sister and it took
Cristo to detach him from her.

'Kiss-do,' Franco warbled mid sob, ready to
smile until Cristo handed him over to the nanny,

and then in desperation stretching his arms out to Belle instead.

Belle moved forward to go to Franco but Cristo forestalled her with a hand on her arm. 'It's our wedding night,' he reminded her drily and the very dryness of his tone disturbed her.

In her opinion only people who loved each other had wedding nights, but that wasn't what she had signed up for, she reminded herself squarely as Cristo led the way along the corridor and cast open a door across yet another landing into a huge bedroom. In spite of her nervousness, the thrill of desire began to build within her.

Belle's attention centred on the giant gilded four-poster bed topped with a gilded coronet and stayed there as if a padlock had snapped her into place. Suddenly she was regretting the innate shyness and mistrust that had kept her out of other men's beds. A little sexual experience would have felt better at that moment when ignorance felt more like a threat.

Cristo closed his arms round her rigid figure

from behind and the scent of him engulfed her. He smelled so good, a citrusy mix of designer cologne and aromatic male that did something strange to her senses. Her heartbeat kicked up pace as he tugged her hair back from her shoulders and bent his mouth to her nape. His chest was against her spine and as solid as rock, and lower down against her bottom she was suddenly startlingly aware that he was aroused and that had the oddest effect on her. Even as her nervous tension heightened, she couldn't help being pleased that she could have that much influence over a male who tended to reveal very little on the surface, and who had stood at the altar in the chapel as though he were an innocent bystander on the brink of boredom.

'I love you in that dress, *gattina mia*,' he growled against her skin, and buried his mouth there in a place she hadn't even known could be sensitive. Every cell in her body pulled taut with anticipation as he laved her flesh with the tip of his tongue and grazed her with the edges of his teeth in an incredibly erotic approach she had certainly not expected from Cristo Ravelli. She was already trembling, her nipples tingling, a sliding sensation of warmth rising between her thighs. A slice of cooler air feathered her spine and her wedding gown slid down her arms without any warning. A gasp of surprise was wrenched from her but ten seconds later the dress was pooled round her feet and he was lifting her out of it.

He spun her round, swiftly engulfing her hands in his before she could make any move to cover the lacy bra, knickers and hold-up stockings she wore beneath. Shimmering eyes, dark as Hades, flared naked gold as they scanned the full curves of her breasts cupped in the bra, sliding down to her narrow waist and the flare of her hips before seguing down the long, shapely length of her legs.

'You were definitely worth waiting for,' Cristo told her with hungry conviction lacing every syllable. 'You're gorgeous, *cara*.'

Belle sucked in a shaken drag of oxygen and then he kissed her with a heat and strength that consumed her. He caressed the seam of her lips, parted them, delved deep and sent a shudder of excitement racing through her that startled her. Yes, as she had noted before, Cristo knew how to kiss and his mouth on hers was deeply addictive and intoxicating. He teased her with his tongue and she shivered and dimly recognised that she was being very efficiently seduced by a man she had once written off as a stuffy banker. Her fingers laced into the thick black hair at the back of his neck and an appreciative growl escaped low in his throat. Just as quickly she became airborne when he scooped her up and settled her down on the bed.

Green eyes dazed, Belle stared back at him, nerves beginning to rise again as he undressed, shedding his tie, his jacket and shoes with a careless haste that flattered her. With his scorching golden eyes pinned to her as intently as though she were Helen of Troy, she realised that he truly did appear to find her very attractive, and when he shed his shirt to reveal six-pack abs and a torso straight out of a male centrefold

Belle's mouth ran dry because for the first time ever *she* was appreciating the male body. With his every movement sleek muscles flexed below smooth golden skin. A thin furrow of dark hair ran from below his navel and disappeared beneath his waistband and then just as quickly he was skimming off the trousers as well, displaying tight buttocks and a…and a massive bulge in the front of his boxers.

At that point, all of Belle's virginal concerns surged to the forefront of her mind. Was he supposed to be that big? Was that normal? She could hardly ask.

Cristo wondered why she was blushing as red as a tomato. He had never seen anything more beautiful or more innately satisfying than the sight of her on top of his bed, clad only in delicate lace lingerie. He tugged off his boxers and left them in a heap, on fire for the climax his body craved.

The full-frontal effect caused Belle to edge back up towards the headboard. He didn't seem to have a single inhibition in his entire body.

Her lashes lowered to screen her expression, heat and what she didn't immediately recognise as hunger snaking through the secret places of her body.

'You're very quiet,' Cristo remarked, tugging her back into the shelter of his arms and reaching behind her to unhook her bra.

'And you're very…single-minded.' Belle selected the word shakily because she thought he had a lot in common with a bullet aimed at a target.

'I've had three weeks to think about this moment,' Cristo growled low in his throat. 'Three weeks too long…I wanted you the first moment I saw you.'

'When you thought I was my mother?' she parried incredulously.

'You were crossing the lawn with the dog in tow and looking exactly like yourself,' Cristo contradicted, raising almost reverent hands to the spill of pale breasts he had unveiled, long fingers tracing the underside of the full round swells. 'You are totally magnificent, *cara mia*.'

Her breath was feathering in and out of her lungs in insufficient drags while he played with her straining nipples, teasing and plucking the tender crowns and sending trickles of fire flaming down into her pelvis. He smoothed his hands down over her quivering frame.

'Are you cold?' he asked in surprise.

'Just a bit nervous,' she gasped, her voice strangled at source as he rested his palm on her inner thigh and then hooked a finger below the lace edge of her knickers and stroked so that a current of pure tingling warmth ran through her veins.

He tipped up her face with his other hand and burning golden eyes assailed hers. 'Why would you be nervous?'

'I haven't done this before.'

'With me,' he filled in.

'With anyone!'

Cristo froze in the midst of trailing off her last garment. 'Are you trying to tell me you're a virgin?'

The heat of mortification flushed her fair skin

like a flaming tide and she couldn't find her voice and was forced to nod affirmation with a jerk of her head.

'And this is not a tease?' Cristo prompted. 'Not a stupid idea to give me what you think could be a wedding-night fantasy?'

Belle focused on him with disconcerted eyes, striving to imagine how he could even suspect such a thing.

Cristo collided with those clear green eyes and discarded his plans of a wedding-night sex marathon. She wouldn't be able to handle that. A virgin. He was good at reading people. He was convinced she wasn't lying and he was shell-shocked because it was not at all what he had expected from her and he did not know whether he liked the idea or not.

'No, not a tease, *cara*,' Cristo said for himself.

'You're disappointed, aren't you?' Belle guessed.

'No, I'm not. You're my wife,' Cristo pointed out with a sudden sense of satisfaction that she would never be able to compare him to another man in bed, never know anything other than what he showed her. A possessive vibe he didn't know he had pulsed through him at that awareness.

'I don't see what difference that makes. I'm not what you expected,' Belle protested.

Still taut with arousal, Cristo was tired of talking. He kissed along her delicate jaw bone and then crushed her generous mouth urgently beneath his, shifting over her to lower his mouth to her generous breasts and then string a line of kisses down over her straining midriff to the very heart of her. He eased a finger into her tight channel and she bucked up her hips and he smiled, loving her responsiveness, parting her thighs for a more intimate caress.

'No…no,' she began, trying to move away.

Glancing up to meet dismayed green eyes, Cristo made a soothing sound he was sure he had never had to make in the bedroom before. 'Trust me…I'll take care of you.'

Belle rested her head back against the pillows and closed her eyes tight, trembling with a crazy mix of mortification laced with tingling sexual awareness and anticipation. He touched her and she gasped out loud because she was so sensitive there and the more he licked and nibbled and tormented her, the more frantically excited she became, all control wrested from her, her body moving in a new feverish rhythm like an instrument being strummed by an expert. Incomprehensible moans and sounds fell from her lips as she writhed and the unbearable ache at her core rose to a crescendo and her whole being was straining towards a climax.

And that was when Cristo lifted over her and eased slowly into the slick, wet welcome of her body. Her eyes flew wide at that shock of sensation, of sudden fullness and stretching inside her.

'This could hurt,' he told her gently.

'I know...' she said breathlessly. 'I'm not a baby.'

For the first time in his life Cristo was more concerned about his partner than himself, which felt strangely alien to him. 'You're so tight,' he bit out, flexing his hips, tipping her up to him for a deeper connection and then sliding home to the very heart of her, causing a stinging, fleeting pain that made her grimace.

'Not too bad,' she told him shakily. 'Just do it.'

Just do it? Cristo laughed out loud and grinned down at her preoccupied face. She looked up at him, rocked by the dark beauty of him at that moment wearing that flashing brilliant smile she had never seen before. And then he moved again, sliding back and delving into her again until he was seated to the hilt and strong sensation was exploding like fireworks inside her. The delicious friction as his hips pounded against hers and the speed of his breathtaking thrusts consumed her with wild excitement. It was electrifyingly intense and passionate and so was he, she registered as her body stiffened and clamped tight around him, and wave after wave of pleasure cascaded through her in a climax so powerful she felt utterly drained in the aftermath but decidedly floaty and full of well-being.

'Well, that was definitely worth getting married for, *bellezza mia*,' Cristo groaned hoarsely in her ear. 'You might be a blackmailer, a gold-digger and a social climber but you're fabulous in bed.'

Belle's eyes flew wide in shock and suddenly she was pushing against those brown muscular shoulders and levering out from underneath him in a rage of disbelief at what he had dared to say to her.

She slid out of the bed like an electrified eel and raced into the bathroom in search of a weapon of mass destruction but there was no club, no gun, no whip, nothing with which to thump him good and hard as pride demanded she must. In desperation she filled a glass by the sink with water and stalked back into the bedroom and slung the contents of the glass at him.

Astonished, Cristo sat up dripping in the tumbled bedding, looking extraordinarily and quite irresistibly handsome with his golden skin and bright eyes and tousled black hair and her awareness of the fact only inflamed her more.

'What the hell?' he demanded, wiping away the water dripping from his face.

'Don't you dare speak to me like that, you pig!' his bride screeched at him like a harpy from his worst nightmares.

'Speak to you…?' For a split second, Cristo frowned. 'Oh…didn't you like me being honest?'

'I am not a blackmailer, a gold-digger or a social climber!' Belle fired at him furiously. 'How dare you accuse me of those things?'

Cristo shot her a derisive look. 'I hate drama queens.'

'You think I care about that? You think I'm ever going to get into that bed again with you after what you called me and the way you spoke to me?' Belle screamed across the depth of the bedroom, so outraged she could barely frame the words.

Cristo lounged back against the banked pillows looking remarkably unconcerned by that threat. 'I think you will because if you *don't*,

I'll be asking for a divorce,' he spelt out without hesitation.

'Right then…I want a divorce!' Belle spat at him before flouncing back into the bathroom and locking shut the door with a loud click.

Well, didn't you handle that well? Cristo reflected, very much in shock himself at what he had divulged to her of his opinions. After all, it wasn't as though such frankness came naturally to him. In fact, Cristo, a man of few words, invariably kept his convictions to himself, but somehow something about that fantastic sex had clashed with his opinion of her inside his head and he had found himself delivering judgement there and then. Had he *wanted* her to know what he thought of her? he queried with a bemused frown. Had he wanted her to prove him wrong or endeavour to develop her character into something more acceptable to him? And why was he even thinking along such lines? He had meant every word he said and he wasn't taking it back or apologising for telling the truth as he saw it.

CHAPTER SIX

ALMOST TWO HOURS later, Cristo scrutinised the empty four-poster bed as if further attention might magically conjure Belle up from below the tossed bedding. His even white teeth clenched so hard his jaw ached. He had gone for a shower in another room, giving her time to settle down, but Belle being Belle, both impulsive and tempestuous, had evidently emerged from the sit-in in the bathroom to take off instead. But to where? It was eleven at night and the palazzo lay several kilometres from the main road.

Cristo expelled his breath with an audible hiss. He had screwed up, screwed up spectacularly and for a reserved and clever male, who rarely ever miscalculated with women, that was a bitter and maddening acknowledgement. Why had he told her what he thought of her and in such terms? That he couldn't answer his own question only made him more angry and unsettled by the experience. It was their wedding night and his bride had run away, not what anyone would call a promising start and for Cristo, who was an irretrievable perfectionist, it was a slap in the face and an unwelcome reminder that he was only human and that humans made mistakes.

At the bottom of the terraced gardens, Belle swung her legs up on her stone bench, striving for a comfort that was unattainable on such an unyielding surface. Unfortunately she could not think of anywhere else to go, certainly not back to the grand building on the top of the hill with its vast and intimidating heavily furnished rooms where she felt like an old-style kitchen maid roaming illicitly from her proper place in the servant's quarters. Oh, Gran, why *didn't* I listen to you? Belle was thinking with feverish regret and an intense sense of self-loathing.

She had married a man who clearly despised her. And worst of all, she had *slept* with him, which just then felt like the biggest self-betrayal of all. Tears dripped silently down Belle's quivering cheeks because she had never felt so alone and out of her depth in her life, at least not since the teenaged years when she had been horrendously bullied. Now she felt trapped, trapped by the marriage, trapped by the promises she had made to her siblings about the wonderful new life ahead of them all. She couldn't just walk away; it wasn't that simple. Telling him she wanted a divorce had been sheer bravado and he had probably recognised it as such.

Cristo Ravelli. He got to her as no other man ever had, rousing feelings and thoughts and reactions she couldn't control. She had become infatuated with him, she decided, mentally and physically infatuated and, as a result, she had acted every bit as foolishly with him as her late mother had once behaved with Gaetano, unable to keep her distance and failing to count the costs of the relationship. How was she supposed to handle Cristo? He was streets ahead of her in the sophistication stakes. He was a

Ravelli, taught from birth that he was a superior being. She hugged her knees, rocking her hips against the hard stone beneath her in an unconscious self-soothing motion, her fingers clenching convulsively together as she fiercely blinked back tears.

Well, the infatuation was dead now. He had *killed* it stone dead. She hated him, absolutely hated him for what he had said within moments of using her body for his pleasure. All right, she reasoned guiltily with herself, it had been *her* pleasure as well. She couldn't pretend to have been an unwilling partner in what had transpired, but then she had not been prepared for that level of passion or pleasure. She had dimly imagined that something much less exciting awaited them in the bedroom.

Mercifully it was a clear night, Cristo conceded grudgingly, tramping down the multitude of steps that featured in the gardens. He was in a filthy mood. Telling Umberto, who ran the palazzo, that his bride was missing had embarrassed him and very little, if anything, embarrassed Cristo. But if he couldn't find Belle, he knew that calling the police in would be considerably *more* embarrassing. He didn't know what he was going to say to her if he *did* find her either. Was he supposed to lie and pretend he hadn't meant his indictment? Apologise for speaking the truth? He was damned if he was going to apologise when she was forcing him to tramp all over his extensive property in search of her in the middle of the night. *Dio mio!* Obviously he was worried about her. Suppose she had come down here in the dark and she had fallen? Hitched a lift out on the country road from some cruising rapist or pervert? Her temper might make her do something self-destructive or dangerous, he reasoned grimly. Cristo's imagination was suddenly travelling in colourful directions it had never gone in before.

And then he heard a noise, the human noise of feet shifting across gravel. *'Belle?'* he called.

Dismay gripping her at the sound of Cristo's voice, Belle returned to her stone bench, having stretched and glued her lips together, but he kept on calling and her silence began to feel childish and selfish and eventually she parted her lips to shout back. 'Go away!'

Relief assailed Cristo. She was safe, would no doubt live to fight many another day with him, a reflection that sent a wash of something oddly like satisfaction through his tall, well-built frame. He followed the voice to its most likely source: the garden pavilion at the very foot of the garden, sited beside a craggy seventeenth-century-built rushing stream and waterfall. Rounding a corner on one of the many paths, he saw her there sitting in darkness, long legs extended in front of her along a stone bench, eyes reflecting the moonlight.

'I was worried about you,' Cristo declared, coming to a halt a couple of feet from the pavilion steps, intimidatingly tall, outrageously assured. 'You didn't answer your cell phone.'

'I don't have it with me and I'm sure you weren't that worried about my welfare,' Belle remarked curtly while quietly noting that he looked more amazing than ever when clad in faded jeans and a casual tee, bare brown feet thrust into leather sandals. 'Not after the way you spoke to me.'

'It was the wrong place, wrong time,' Cristo admitted, mounting the steps to lift the lighter from its hook on the wall and ignite the fat pillar candle in the centre of the stone table.

Not even slightly soothed by that comeback, Belle tilted her chin as the candle flame illuminated his darkly handsome features while he looked down at her from the opposite side of the table. 'But it was obviously what you thought… *blackmail*?'

'I did tell you that other people could be seriously embarrassed by you taking such a story to court on your siblings' behalf,' Cristo reminded her stubbornly. 'You told me you didn't care.'

Your siblings, not his as well, she noted in exasperation, since he was clearly still set on denying that blood tie. 'Why should I have? Neither you nor your brothers care about them.'

'Neither Nik nor Zarif even know of your siblings' existence as yet,' Cristo pointed out.

'Nik's not into children though. For Zarif, how-ever, the news that throughout the whole of his parents' marriage Gaetano was sleeping with another woman and having a tribe of children with her would be deeply destructive and dam-aging. He's the new King of Vashir.'

Belle rolled her eyes, unimpressed or, at least, *trying* to seem unimpressed. 'I know that.'

'Vashir is a very devout and conservative so-ciety and Gaetano's behaviour would cause a huge scandal there, which would engulf Zar-if's image in Gaetano's sleaze. Every ruler has opponents and it would be used against him to remind people that his father was a foreigner with a sordid irreligious lifestyle. He doesn't deserve that. Like all of us, he paid the price of having Gaetano as a father while he was still a child,' Cristo informed her grimly. 'I offered to marry you and adopt those children to prevent that from happening.'

'But you didn't tell me that, so you can hardly expect me to be sympathetic now,' Belle told him roundly. 'It's not only a little late in the day to start calling me a blackmailer, it's also darned unfair when you never gave me those facts in the first place!'

At that spirited retort, Cristo gritted his teeth again in smouldering silence.

'I did *not* blackmail you!' Belle exclaimed, sliding off the bench to stand up and walk down the steps before turning back to face him while his attention lingered on her slender leggy proportions in the denim shorts and camisole she wore. 'Evidently my plans to go to court on the children's behalf put you between a rock and a hard place but *you* made the decision to propose marriage!'

Lean, strong features set in forbidding lines in the shadowy candlelight, Cristo stared broodingly back at her. 'I did but even now I know that your plans to have your day in court would have damaged those children more than you can possibly appreciate.'

'You don't know what you're talking about!'

'I know *exactly* what I'm talking about—in fact nobody knows better!' Cristo parried with unexpected rawness, his dark eyes glittering like stars. 'Gaetano trailed my mother through court in a supposed attempt to gain custody of me when I was a child. Of course what he really wanted was a bigger payoff from the divorce. He didn't want me; he never wanted me. All the dirty secrets of my parents' marriage were trailed out in court and made headlines across Europe and you can *still* read about it online if you know where to look. Do you really think those children would thank you either now or years from now for seeing their parents' less than stellar private life splashed across the tabloids and the net?'

That angle hadn't occurred to Belle and she gulped. 'Naturally I didn't want your charity when the children were legally entitled to a share in their own name.'

'It wouldn't have been charity.'

'No, but you would've been buying my silence and theirs!' she lashed back at him angrily. 'I watched what you did with Mayhill—all aboard the Ravelli gravy train to keep everyone quiet about Gaetano, Mary and their kids.'

'Didn't you climb aboard the same train with a wedding ring?' Cristo taunted with sizzling derision.

'No, I darned well didn't!' Belle hurled back, temper leaping up in a surge of inner flame. 'Because no matter what you think I'm *not* a gold-digger or a social climber! I married you for the sake of my brothers and sisters, so that they would never have to go through what Bruno and I went through!'

'What did you go through?' Cristo demanded with galling impatience.

'When Mum started the affair with Gaetano and then later when she gave birth to Bruno, I think people were inclined to turn a blind eye to it all because everybody knew she'd had a rough time with my father until he died.' Belle breathed in deep, angry pain and mortification coursing through her slender length. 'Back then the locals felt sorry for her—my father was an abusive drunk.'

'And then?' Cristo's attention was locked to her beautiful face and the glistening lucidity of her wide green eyes.

'And then it went sour for all of us because Mum continued the affair with Gaetano and went on having children. Everyone knew Gaetano had a wife abroad. They decided Mum was shameless and bold and stopped talking to her, wouldn't even serve her in some village shops,' Belle recounted unhappily. 'But she lived in the Lodge outside the village and shopped elsewhere so the hostility didn't really touch her...but I went to local schools with the children of those judgemental parents...'

Her voice momentarily ran out of steam and then picked up again as she shared a memory, a haunted look on her face as if she had drifted mental miles away, and in a way she had because she was back there, walking into a classroom as a vulnerable adolescent, being called a slut by a bunch of girls because everyone knew her mother was a woman who had just given birth to two more children by her married lover.

Nobody had intervened when she was bullied because it was widely known and accepted that Mary Brophy was a wicked woman raising her children in a degenerate home where the most basic rules of morality and decency were being broken on a regular basis.

'I never had any friends apart from Mark,' she admitted curtly. 'The other mothers wouldn't let their daughters mix with me or come to my house. It got worse as I got older because then I had the boys calling me names as well and making approaches…well, you can imagine the approaches.'

Cristo, raised from an early age in a city that bred anonymity, was genuinely taken aback by what she was telling him. He'd had no suspicion of the moral rectitude in a small rural community where those who dared to defy public opinion and break the rules could be punished by exclusion and enmity.

'I didn't want my sisters or my brothers to go through that.'

'Obviously not, *cara*,' Cristo murmured ruefully, suddenly grasping one very good reason why his bride had been inexperienced because she had naturally been denied that outlet as a teenager and young woman when to give way to the desire to experiment could have surely seen her labelled as having followed in her mother's footsteps. 'And Bruno?'

'I'll tell you about that some other time but he was bullied as well. That's why he and Donetta were sent to boarding school in the first place.'

'Are you coming back up to the house?' Cristo enquired in the dragging silence that had fallen. 'It *is* two o'clock in the morning.'

Belle prayed for calm and restraint as she walked away from the pavilion. 'You were very offensive and insulting…and disrespectful too.'

'*Sì, bellezza mia*, but it is possible that complete honesty could be the best way forward in a marriage such as ours,' Cristo stated thoughtfully.

Belle mulled that concept over while she mounted yet another endless flight of steps. All the emotion and activity of the day were suddenly hitting her in one go and exhaustion was weighing her down. 'I haven't forgiven you, though,' she was quick to tell him, lest he be assuming that the slate had been wiped clean when it wasn't.

Having watched her pace flag, Cristo closed an arm round her slender spine to guide her up the steep incline. 'That's okay.'

Cristo felt surprisingly buoyant as he urged her back upstairs to their bedroom. In the light he could see the marks of tearstains on her face and his conscience pierced his tough hide. She was so much more emotional than he was and that unnerved him. He would never forget the wounded expression on her face when she had told him about the bullying she had endured at school. To his way of thinking, her mother had been every bit as selfish in her own way as his father, he reflected grimly, but he knew better than to share that thought.

At the same time, he could only be impressed by how very protective Belle was of her brothers and sisters. He had never known that family intimacy, never appreciated that love could bond a family so tightly together, and he could not help wondering how different he might have been had he shared a similar experience. In spite of the misfortunes Gaetano had caused Mary Brophy's children, they remained a very closely connected unit.

'I'm not getting back into the same bed,' Belle announced one step inside the bedroom door.

Payback time, Cristo acknowledged. 'I'm not that insensitive. I wasn't about to make a move on you.'

Her eyes were prickling with the sudden heat of tears and she held them wide to hold the tears back. 'I know, but I still need my own space for a while,' she said tightly.

Cristo searched the pale, unhappy tightness of her lovely face and compressed his stubborn mouth, knowing without even thinking about it that he didn't want her away from him and, even worse, had a disturbing desire to keep her close. 'I'd prefer you to stay with me.'

Mere minutes later, having won that last battle, Belle settled heavy as a stone into the comfortable bed in the room next door and lowered her lashes on her damp eyes. She had wanted to be with him but had angrily denied herself that choice because common sense had told her it would be wrong. Wrong to let Cristo think he could do and say as he liked without consequences, wrong to let him hurt her and then put a brave face on it to the extent that he would think he might as well do it again. *Blackmailer, gold-digger, social climber?* Was it even possible for her to disprove such suspicions? And should she even want to? Did it really matter? After all, theirs was a marriage of convenience and she simply had to learn to keep a better hold on her emotions and stop looking for responses she was unlikely to receive. She couldn't afford to start caring about a male who didn't care about her but, regardless of every other factor, she was utterly determined that, at the very least, Cristo would give her respect.

Cristo lay sleepless in bed and expelled a groan. He knew Belle was treating him just as she treated Franco with the 'no means no' approach and the withdrawal of privileges until better behaviour was established. In the darkness he suddenly surprised himself when amusement surged over him and he laughed out loud. She had thrown him a challenge. No woman had ever done that to Cristo before and it bothered him to appreciate that he actually admired her nerve.

The next morning, Cristo wakened when something bounced hard on the bed and his eyes flew wide on the dawn light piercing the curtains.

'Kiss-do!' Franco carolled from below his mop of black curls and looked down expectantly at him. *'Belle?'*

'Belle's asleep,' Cristo responded, anchoring the sheet more firmly round his naked length as Franco threw his small solid body at him. 'Bekfast?' Franco asked hopefully, leaning over him with wide eyes.

Wondering where the nanny was, Cristo promised breakfast and Franco beamed. Indeed, Cristo was startled when his little brother wound his arms round his neck and bestowed a soggy kiss on him. The toddler accompanied him into the en suite, chattering endlessly but using few recognisable words. Cristo showered and shaved while Franco played with the contents of the drawers and cupboards and made an unholy mess. While he got dressed, Franco played under the bed with, 'Bekfast, Kiss-do?' a constant refrain to the activity.

Franco closed his hand into Cristo's as they left the bedroom and the flustered nanny appeared several doors further down the corridor.

'I'm so sorry, Mr Ravelli. I've been looking everywhere for him. He disappeared while I was in the bathroom,' Teresa confided.

'Relax, I'll ensure he gets breakfast.'

'Bekfast,' Franco repeated urgently, swinging on Cristo's hand and skipping with excitement. There was a definite charm to the child's open-hearted affection and liveliness, Cristo conceded reluctantly.

In the dining room, Umberto provided an ancient wooden high chair for Franco's use and Cristo advised the manservant to see that a new one was purchased with a safety harness because he was already aware that Franco was an escape artist and guilty of frequently climbing out of his cot. Whatever Cristo ate, Franco wanted to eat and Cristo was quietly appalled at the mess the child made. When he threw a piece of tomato, Cristo told him off and Franco burst into floods of tears, which had to be the exact moment when Belle entered the room.

'Oh, my goodness, I didn't know he was with you!' Belle gasped in dismay.

'He's a very determined little character,' Cristo remarked above the racket Franco was making. 'I told him off for throwing food.'

'No hug, then,' Belle ruled as Franco held out his arms to be comforted. 'You know you're not allowed to throw food.'

Franco sulked when his complaints were ignored and finally started eating again.

Belle grinned across the table at Cristo. 'Thanks for looking after him.'

The natural glory of her smile took his breath away and his dark eyes narrowed appreciatively. It was first thing in the morning and as far as he could tell she wasn't wearing much make-up but she still looked amazing, her translucent china skin flushed and freckled, green eyes bright, her mane of hair coiling round her slim shoulders with a life all of its own in every bouncy corkscrew curl of auburn. 'He's my brother as well,' Cristo murmured wryly. 'And quite a handful.'

'Yes, he is…far too much for Isa to cope with at this age.' Pleased by that long-awaited concession that Franco was *his* brother too, Belle stared at Cristo, trying to stop herself from doing it but quite unable to resist the temptation. Her gaze traced the line of his high-cut cheekbones, perfectly straight nose and wide shapely mouth. The perfect features of a dark fallen angel, which got to her every time. A rush of heat tightened her nipples and surged low in her pelvis in a betrayal she could not squash. She still found him irresistibly attractive, she conceded ruefully.

The thwack-thwack of noisy helicopter rotor blades somewhere nearby made Cristo frown and spring upright to stride over to the window. Still munching her toast, Belle followed suit. 'What is it?'

'I think you're about to make the acquaintance of one of my brothers,' Cristo murmured tautly. 'Nik. Make allowances for him if he's short with you. He's going through a tough divorce and it's unsettled him.'

'I'll just make myself scarce while you catch up with him,' Belle offered, hastily lifting Franco out of the elderly high chair.

'No, he should meet you now that he's here, *gioia mia*,' Cristo overruled without hesitation. 'You're my wife. I'm not ashamed of you, nor am I going to hide you.'

CHAPTER SEVEN

CRISTO STRODE OUTSIDE to greet his brother, Nik. The two men stopped on the terrace to talk. Belle hovered, hearing an animated exchange between the men in a foreign language. It didn't sound like Italian and she wondered if it could be Greek. When she heard the other man expostulate loudly several times she guessed that Cristo was telling him about her mother and the children and she winced uncomfortably, feeling agonisingly self-conscious.

Nik Christakis was a big man, even taller than her bridegroom, but he did bear a strong resemblance to Cristo. Nik frowned across the room at her and his frown only darkened more when he saw the young child standing by her side.

'My wife, Belle, and our youngest little brother, Franco,' Cristo imparted in calm explanation in response to his brother's interrogative look. 'My brother, Nik.'

'*Our?*' Nik queried straight away. 'The child's nothing to do with me. Five of them? You would have to be crazy to take that on, Cristo! Gaetano's dead and buried. What does it matter what comes out about him now?'

'It would matter to Zarif,' Cristo countered squarely.

'Like I care about that!' Nik quipped darkly, digging into an inside pocket on his jacket to extract a document, which he extended to his brother. 'Read it and weep. Learn what happens when you get married without a pre-nup.'

'We didn't have a pre-nup,' Belle remarked awkwardly, uneasy with the tension flowing around them, and Nik's reluctance to even acknowledge her, never mind make polite conversation.

Cristo raised his dark gaze slowly from the document to say, 'I have to admit that I'm surprised.'

'Are you? Are you still that naïve? Obviously

Betsy married me for my money and now she's trying to steal half of everything I own!' Nik declared with raw, unconcealed bitterness.

'She *didn't* marry you for your money,' Cristo contradicted with quiet assurance. 'She fell in love with you.'

'Don't be naïve. I give you and your wife and her little bunch of Ravelli by-blows two years at most before she walks out and tries to take the shirt off your back!' Nik vented with ringing derision.

Belle flushed and lifted her chin. 'I wouldn't do that. Look, I'll leave you two to talk in private,' she completed, anchoring Franco's hand in her own.

As she left she heard Nik Christakis cursing, something that was instantly recognisable in many languages. She realised that she was very grateful not to be married to a man like that. Nik's hard-featured face, cold eyes, not to mention the smouldering bitterness that escaped every time he mentioned his estranged wife, Betsy, chilled Belle to the marrow. Nik was clearly tough, obstinate, furiously hostile and, she suspected, the sort of man who would make an implacable enemy, a man who saw only the worst in anyone who crossed him.

Cristo, she reasoned, was more reasonable, more civilised...wasn't he? She respected him for speaking up in defence of his sister-in-law. Furthermore the night before she had been surprised and reluctantly impressed when Cristo had suggested that complete honesty between them might well be the way to make their marriage work. That was a rational and mature attitude to take, she acknowledged thoughtfully. She liked and respected honesty, hated the lies and persuasive pretences that Gaetano had shamelessly employed to keep her mother content and make his own life smoother.

Two hours later, after Nik had finally departed and a second helicopter had flown in and deposited its colourful cargo, Cristo went off in search of Belle and found her sitting in the shade of a tree clutching a book. 'You own a massive library of books,' she complained as she heard his approach and lifted her head, auburn hair gleaming rich as silk in the shadowy light below the overhanging foliage, 'but I could only find a couple written in English.'

Cristo swiped the hardback from between her fingers and studied the spine. It was a heavy-duty tome on the history of his mother's family, written by one of his ancestors and translated by a more recent one. 'I'll order some English books for you. I'd suggest that you start learning Italian but it would hardly be worth your while.'

Her bone structure tightened, tension leaping through her as she absorbed that reminder that their relationship was of a strictly temporary nature. Images of his passionate lovemaking the night before swam up through her mind and killed every sensible thought stone dead, making concentration impossible while sending a wave of unwelcome heat travelling through her slender length. Her face hot, she studied the book fixedly as he returned it to her with an elegant gesture of one long-fingered hand. Last night those hands had touched her with breathtakingly erotic expertise and had extracted more pleasure from her weak body than she had known it was capable of experiencing. His complete poise in the aftermath of their passionate argument the night before, however, set her teeth firmly on edge. Evidently, as far as he was concerned, everything was done and dusted but Belle still felt as though her reactions, emotions and even her thoughts were whirling around in a maelstrom and out of her control.

'Were you looking for me?' she asked curiously.

'Yes, *cara*. It's time for you to enjoy your wedding present.'

'Wedding present?' Belle parroted as she rose slowly to her feet in discomfiture. 'What on earth are you talking about?'

'Wedding presents go with the territory of getting married,' Cristo fielded smoothly, a lean hand settling to the base of her spine to steer her back in the direction of the villa.

'But not between us, not in *our* sort of marriage,' she parried with spirit.

'I promised to treat you as my wife and that is what I am trying to do.'

'So…' Belle murmured tightly in the echoing hall. 'This present…?'

'It's waiting for you in the ballroom,' Cristo informed her, nodding to Umberto to open the double doors.

Belle crossed the hall slowly, peering into the vast room to focus in astonishment on the catwalk now dissecting it. 'My goodness, what the heck—?' she began in confusion.

'Every woman wants a new wardrobe. I arranged to have a selection flown in along with the models to show the clothing off. All you have to do is choose what you want to wear.'

Every woman wants a new wardrobe? Most social climbing, gold-digging women would certainly fall into that category, Belle reflected with a helpless little moue of distaste that he should have assumed that she was that sort of a woman. But he hadn't given her a choice. This was what Cristo thought she wanted and, it seemed, he was happy to deliver on that score and it would be needlessly confrontational for her to deny him the opportunity. One step into the ballroom she was introduced to Olivia, who whisked a tape measure over her with startling speed and efficiency and announced that any garments she selected would be delivered sized to fit by lunchtime the next day.

Funky music kicked off in the background as Olivia took one of three comfortable seats awaiting them while urging Belle to define what Olivia described as 'her personal style'. Belle had to hinge her jaw closed at the question because she had no idea how to answer it. In any case Olivia had already embarked on a commentary on the first outfit while a brunette model wearing something floaty, purple and weirdly shaped like a lampshade strolled down the catwalk towards them. As a very tall blonde with a shock of almost-white chopped hair appeared in swimwear Olivia endeavoured to determine Belle's fashion preferences. But Belle had never had the budget to develop a taste for luxury. As a student, she had worn jeans in winter and shorts in summer with only the occasional cheap skirt or dress purchased for nights out. Money had always been in short supply in her life, clothing generally purchased from her part-time earnings as a bartender, and she had only ever shopped in chain stores.

'Don't you like any of it?' Cristo prompted, shooting his bride a questioning glance from his brooding dark eyes when she remained awkwardly silent.

As she connected with his stunning eyes her heart flipped inside her chest and turned a somersault. 'It's a bit overwhelming…all this,' she admitted breathlessly.

'Then I'll choose for you.'

And *what* Cristo chose was highly informative and Belle almost burst out laughing, for without fail every short skirt, backless gown and low neckline received Cristo's unqualified and enthusiastic vote of approval. On that score he was very predictable, very male and reassuringly human. Amused by the very basic male he was revealing beneath the sophisticated façade, Belle began to regain her confidence and started to quietly voice opinions, shying away from the more spectacular garments in favour of the plainer ones, insisting that she couldn't possibly wear shocking pink with her hair.

'I like pink,' Cristo argued without hesitation. Though as Olivia took up the conversation he suddenly remembered his feelings of horror at the many shades of pink spun throughout the small home back in Ireland. But his *wife* in pink…that was a different matter.

'There are only certain shades of pink which you should avoid,' Olivia, ever the highly accomplished saleswoman, assured her.

At that point the blonde appeared in a ravishing set of ruffled turquoise lingerie and Cristo sprang upright and actually approached the catwalk. 'I want that,' he spelt out without an ounce of discomfiture in his bearing.

Belle's cheeks flamed while she noted the manner in which the very leggy blonde was posing for Cristo like a stripper, loving the attention as her breasts jiggled in the bra with her little dance movements, and she spun round to display her almost bare bottom taut in panties that were little more than a thong. Cristo seemed mesmerised by the spectacle, his dark golden eyes veiled, his sinfully seductive bronzed features taut as if he was struggling to conceal his thoughts.

He was attracted to the blonde, Belle decided with a sinking sick sensation in the pit of her stomach, and he couldn't hide the fact.

'Thank you, Sofia,' the saleswoman said loudly as she stood up and the music stopped mid-note, leaving a sudden uncomfortable silence in its wake. Olivia said her goodbyes and took her leave through the rear door of the ballroom.

'Well, wasn't that educational?' Belle remarked freezingly when Cristo finally wandered back to her side.

His winged ebony brows drew together in bewilderment. 'How so?'

Her generous mouth compressed. 'You fancied the blonde,' she told him bluntly.

Cristo frowned.

'Oh, don't bother denying it. I saw you,' Belle told him thinly. 'You couldn't take your eyes off her!'

Cristo moved steadily closer in a slow stalking movement that was quite ridiculously sensual. Belle looked up at him, fearless in her condemnation, and collided with smouldering golden eyes so intense in focus that she was rocked back on her heels. All the oxygen in the atmosphere seemed to have dried up and she parted her lips to snatch in air.

'I have only one point to make. It wasn't her I was seeing…it was *you*,' he spelt out hoarsely, his brilliant eyes pinned to her with mesmerising force. 'It was *you* I was picturing in that get-up.'

Disbelief assailed Belle and she flicked him a scornful upward glance of dismissal. 'Like I'm going to believe that with a half-naked beauty cavorting in front of you!' she derided.

'*Believe*...' Cristo urged in a roughened undertone that vibrated with assurance in the stillness. 'When I've got a real woman like you, why would I want one with fewer curves than a coat hanger?'

Her mouth fell wide at that less than flattering description of the beautiful model. 'Not your type?'

'You're my type,' Cristo confided huskily. 'The erotic image of you bountifully filling those little blue scraps of nothing turns me on fast and hard.'

A *real* woman? Belle almost laughed out loud at that label. After all, the rigorous dieting she had tried in her teen years had failed to hone an inch off the solid bone structure that gave her defiantly curvaceous hips and voluptuous breasts. Back then she would have given her right arm to be one of the more fashionable 'skinny-minnies' at school. But she was not fool enough as an adult to instantly dismiss the idea that some men actually preferred curves to more slender proportions. It simply hadn't entered her head before that Cristo might be one of those men.

He brushed a straying curl from her cheek and tucked it behind her ear with a casual intimacy that unnerved her. It said that he had the right to touch her, a right she had already denied him. An alarm bell shrieked in her brain, warning her to back off and enforce her boundaries yet again. But he was close, *so* temptingly close that she could smell the evocative scent of cologne and masculine musk that he emanated. He smelt so unbelievably good to her that her senses swam and she felt light-headed. Her knees wobbled beneath her while warmth snaked down from the breasts straining below her camisole to the very core of her, leaving her feeling hot and achy and dissatisfied. Even staying still in that condition was a challenge.

He touched her face, a long tanned forefinger gently tracing the line of her jaw to the cupid's bow above her upper lip while a thumb stroked the soft fullness of her lower lip. Belle trembled, scarcely able to breathe for the rush of excitement that had come out of nowhere at her. Her body raced up the scale in reaction, temperature rising, heart pounding, pulse hammering. Her lashes lowered to a languorous half-mast as she gazed up at him in helpless silence, for she had no words to describe what he was doing to her. He was so beautiful, so devastatingly beautiful that she hadn't even blamed the models for concentrating their attention on him while they displayed their wares. Not only was he the buyer, but also a male so handsome that he made women stare while they struggled to comprehend what it was about those lean, darkly dazzling features that exercised such sinful power and magnetism over their sex. Belle didn't know; she only knew that the minute she stopped looking at him, she *needed* to look again. It was a compulsion she couldn't fight.

'You can put on that blue set just for me,'

Cristo murmured hungrily, stunning dark eyes flaring wicked gold at that prospect.

'In your dreams,' Belle warned him without hesitation, thinking he would wait a very long time if he hoped to see her tricked out in provocative underwear for his benefit. Playing the temptress wasn't her style and in her opinion he didn't need the encouragement. That conviction in mind, she walked into the drawing room, where at least their conversation would be unheard by the staff.

'Don't tell me that you don't have the same dream,' Cristo chided, shifting in front of her to clamp his lean hands possessively to her hips.

Belle was about to hit him, push him away, stamp on his foot, loudly lodge a protest to physical contact of any kind. She really was going to do at least one of those things and then his mouth plunged down hungrily on hers and her hands spread against the hard, warm contours of his chest and slowly fisted into the fabric of his shirt as she fought herself and fought the craving he induced.

In that split second between her thinking and acting, his tongue snaked into her mouth to taste her and she was lost while he nipped and teased at her lips and delved deep. The hot, throbbing sensation between her legs rose in intensity until she was rocking her hips against his, wanting more, *needing* more with an urgency that unnerved her. She could feel the long, hard ridge of his arousal against her belly and their clothes were an obstruction she couldn't bear, overwhelming physical hunger surging through her quivering body with a force she couldn't withstand.

Cristo lifted his handsome head, eyes hot and bright with sexual heat, black hair tousled by the fingers she had dug into the luxuriant strands, an edge of colour accentuating his hard cheekbones. 'Shall we take this upstairs?' he murmured thickly.

No was on Belle's lips but yes was in her heart because her body was drenched with treacherous longing for his. She took in a slow steadying breath and struggled to clear her head, fighting the wanting clawing at her with all her strength.

'I want you...you want me, *cara,*' Cristo said drily. 'What's the problem? Are you still suspicious about that model? Do you really think I'd be that crass?'

'No,' Belle conceded reluctantly, for she would have used that as an excuse had she been able to do so. Unfortunately, her brain was in free fall. He had spoken the truth: the attraction between them was explosive. Furthermore, had he not been strongly attracted to her in the first place, he probably wouldn't have offered her marriage. Even so the bond that was being created between them solely on a physical level was too superficial for her to accept and she wanted more.

Cristo elevated a sleek black brow. '*Then?* Are you still judging me as if I'm my late father?' he demanded impatiently. 'Or is it something in your own past which makes you so suspicious of men?'

Belle stiffened. 'I don't know what you're talking about—'

'I think you do. You watched Gaetano run rings round your mother and hated him for it,' Cristo contended. 'But I'm *not* him.'

Belle bridled and gritted her teeth. 'I know that and I didn't say you were.'

'Why else would you accuse me of coming on to that model right in front of you?' Cristo slung back, tension etched along the hard line of his cheekbones and the angle of his strong jawline. 'What sort of a man would behave like that?'

'I overreacted. I'm sorry.' Belle turned her vibrant head away, guilt and mortification piercing her. There was a certain amount of truth to his condemnation. She did distrust men but not *all* men. During her years at university she had been hurt by boyfriends who were offended by her refusal to get straight into bed with them before she even got to know them. The same boys had deceived her with other girls and let her down but no more so than any of her friends, who had suffered similar wake-up calls from young men who wanted nothing more lasting from a woman than physical release.

'If you want this marriage to work, this isn't the way to go about it,' Cristo delivered in a measured undertone.

'You said honesty was the best policy,' Belle reminded him, walking away a few steps and then turning back to face him, her lovely face flushed and tense. 'Then I'll *be* honest. For this to work for me, I want something more than just sex with you. I want us to get to know each other. You can't build a relationship purely on sex.'

'I've never known anything else,' Cristo growled.

'Do you have any female friends?'

When he nodded with a faint frown, Belle smiled. 'Well, then, you have known something else.'

'Why didn't you make these demands *before* you married me?' Cristo derided.

'I didn't think it through until now,' Belle confided truthfully. 'I was desperate to make the children secure and marrying you was the price. I didn't think beyond that. I didn't think about how I would *feel*...'

Marrying you was the price. Not a statement he had expected to hear from Belle, not one he was even sure he could believe, Cristo mused grimly, dark eyes shielded by his lush lashes. She wanted more. Why did women always want more than was on offer? Were they pro-grammed to want more at birth? All this and five children too, he reflected heavily—had he really thought about what he was doing either?

The forbidding look tensing his lean, dark fea-tures stirred Belle's conscience. 'I realise this is coming out of nowhere at you and you have a right to be irritated.'

'That's not quite the word I would've chosen,' Cristo countered curtly.

Belle steeled herself to be more honest than she really wanted to be. 'I *did* have thoughts I shouldn't have had when I agreed to marry you,' she admitted gruffly, her pale skin suddenly blossoming with mortified colour. 'But none of those thoughts related to personal enrichment or social advancement.' Feeling more uncomfortable than ever, she hesitated. 'Although I wouldn't go as far as to say that I had thoughts of getting revenge for what Gaetano put my family through over the years, I certainly had an inappropriate sense of satisfaction when you offered to marry me and I quite deliberately wore my mother's wedding dress to get married in. I'm ashamed of those feelings now. After all, it was very unfair that you should have to pay in any way for your father's mistakes. But then we're both doing that now,' she completed ruefully.

Cristo was violently disconcerted by her complete honesty. He hadn't expected that, hadn't been prepared for her to admit any reactions that might reflect badly on her motivation in marrying him. Getting a rich and powerful Ravelli to the altar had briefly thrilled her but she had owned up to it and that impressed a male who was rarely impressed by the women he met.

'*La via dell'inferno è lastricata di buone intenzione*…the road to hell is paved with good intentions,' Cristo translated sibilantly. 'Do you ever do anything for the sheer hell of it?'

'No.' Belle stiffened as she made that admission. 'And it doesn't have to be hell,' she pointed out uncomfortably. 'We can make the best of the situation. You said you wanted to treat me like a proper wife, wanted to show me respect…'

The reminder hung there like a dark cloud between them, with Cristo finally registering that his partiality for that lingerie set had evidently caused offence. Last night he had become her first lover and she had been *amazing*, he recalled, arousal slivering through him at even the memory. He was expecting too much too soon and he gritted his perfect white teeth together. 'I'll try harder,' he told her in a driven undertone.

'I'll try too,' Belle responded with a tentative smile.

But it was too late because Cristo had already turned away and could not have seen her smile, which had combined both regret at her inability to be the purely sexual object he so clearly wanted her to be and her hope for a better understanding between them in the future. Spirits low, she went upstairs to find her little brother and give Teresa a break. Franco's warm affection and trusting acceptance that he would be loved back were wonderfully soothing to her troubled state of mind. She played hide and seek with the little boy and the upper floor rang with laughter and thudding feet.

Umberto paused in Cristo's office doorway to say warmly, 'It is a joy to hear a child playing here again.'

'There's another four of them—a boy and a girl of eight and a pair of teenagers,' Cristo confided, for he had known the kindly manservant since he was a child.

'Your late father's children?' Umberto prompted.

Cristo's brows drew together. 'How did you know?'

'I heard rumours over the years. My cousin

flew Mr Gaetano's helicopter right up until his retirement,' the older man reminded him gently.

'Let's hope the rumours stay buried,' Cristo commented wryly.

'No one in my family will gossip,' the older man assured him with pride. 'But Mr Gaetano had other staff who may not be so discreet.'

A current of uneasiness assailed Cristo, who had ensured that his father's surviving employees were paid off with adequate remuneration for their years of service. Was it possible he had got married for no good reason? And inexplicably, at that point, he thought of Franco, who demonstrated such a desperate need for male attention. Franco definitely needed a father figure, Cristo reflected, his stern mouth softening as the toddler's gales of laughter echoed down from above.

'No…no…*no*, Franco!' Belle gasped in dismay when she found her little brother picking in delight through the collection of items lying on the dressing table in Cristo's bedroom. 'Don't touch those.'

Jingling the car keys still in his hand, Franco dropped the wallet he had been investigating and it fell to the floor. Belle knelt down to gather up the banknotes that Franco had crumpled, smoothing them out before returning them to the wallet along with credit cards, a couple of business cards and…a tiny photograph. Belle lifted the photo and stared down at it in surprise, recognising Nik Christakis's estranged wife, Betsy. She was a little blonde sprite of a beauty with delicate features and big blue eyes. Her brow furrowed. Had the photo fallen out of the wallet or had it just been lying there forgotten on the floor? The rug beneath her knees, however, bore the ruffled evidence of recent vacuuming. So, assuming the photo *had* been inside Cristo's wallet, why was her husband carrying round a photo of his brother's wife?

And was she even going to ask him why? Belle came out in a cold sweat at the very prospect of so embarrassing a conversation. After her misjudgement of his behaviour with the model, he would never believe that she had accidentally seen the photograph. He would think she had been snooping in his wallet and he would naturally assume that she was one of those madly jealous, distrustful women, who would always be scheming to check his cellphone messages and his pockets for evidence of infidelity. Cringing at that likelihood, Belle slotted the photo back into his wallet and returned it circumspectly to the dressing table. No, she wasn't about to ask him any more awkward questions.

Matters were tense enough between them. And yet so many important things hinged on the success of their marriage, she thought wretchedly. If she and Cristo couldn't make a go of it, what would happen to her siblings? She had made promises, not least those in the chapel, which she had to, at least, *try* to keep. Unless she was prepared to let Cristo go free, she had to make more of an effort.

But please, no, she prayed, let not the only avenue to success demand the sporting of saucy underwear....

CHAPTER EIGHT

BELLE SAT ALONE at the breakfast table out on
the terrace, which overlooked the glorious gardens and, beyond them, the beautiful panorama
of the idyllic Umbrian landscape, and decided
that nobody would ever credit how miserable
and insecure she was. Here she was, all dressed
up in gorgeous surroundings, married to an
even more gorgeous man and already she had
made a mess of things! Although, to be fair,
expecting her to be willing to put on provocative lingerie for his benefit had scarcely been
calculated to soothe her misgivings.

*Do you ever do anything for the sheer hell of
it?* Cristo had asked. And the truthful answer
would have been, no, *never.* So, how on earth
had she managed to leap into marrying Cristo
without fully considering what she was doing?
She still couldn't answer that question to her

own satisfaction. Had her treacherous attraction to him destroyed every single one of her brain cells? Why hadn't she listened to her grandmother's warnings? After all, nobody knew better than Belle that relationships between men and women were often difficult and prone to unhappiness.

Her mother's over-hasty marriage at a young age to Belle's drunken father followed by Mary's long affair with Gaetano Ravelli had taught Belle to be very cautious and sensible and to carefully reason out every move she made in advance with men, *except* when it came to the opportunity to marry Cristo when she had—inexplicably to her—jumped right in with both feet. And her current wary attitude to intimacy was creating friction with Cristo. Could she blame him for his outlook?

What, after all, had Cristo *gained* from their marriage? Her silence, no court case and five pretty needy children he had promised to adopt into the Ravelli family. Her tense mouth downcurved on the discouraging suspicion that he had sacrificed much more than she had and that few people would feel sorry for her having given up her freedom to work and instead live in the lap of luxury with her fancy designer wardrobe. That thought made her eyes sting fiercely with tears because she had very little interest in the luxury and the vast selection of new clothes that had been delivered in garment bags to her room before she even got out of bed. In fact, she had only donned one of the outfits, a silky top and skirt, because she hadn't wanted Cristo to think that she was ungrateful for the gesture he had made.

But unfortunately, Cristo wasn't even around to notice what she was wearing. That was the problem of separate bedrooms in a massive house and two people who didn't know each other's habits very well, Belle reflected wretchedly. Cristo had been absent at dinner the night before and now he was absent again. Was he avoiding her? Fed up with her immature outlook? It seemed pretty obvious to her that she was getting absolutely everything in their marriage wrong, and to achieve that at such an early stage suggested that she had cherished completely unreasonable expectations of what being married to Cristo would entail. He had assumed she was a gold-digger and, having brooded over that accusation, she wasn't sure she could blame him for his cynicism. After all, he didn't know her and possibly connecting on a physical level was the only way Cristo knew *how* to get to know a woman, so her coming over all prudish and standoffish because he had hurt her feelings wasn't helping the situation…

And worst of all, Belle knew she couldn't even phone her grandmother. Isa Kelly's sensible advice would have been very welcome even though Belle could not have brought herself to mention the bedroom side of things to the older woman. Indeed even the sound of Isa's voice and those of her siblings would have been a comfort. Belle was horribly homesick and missed the family dog, Tag, almost as much. But Belle knew that if she phoned home within days of the wedding her grandmother would be astute enough to suspect that things weren't working out and it would be very, very selfish to lay yet another worry on her grandmother's already overburdened shoulders.

Disgusted at her self-pitying mood and lack of activity, Belle suddenly pushed her chair back and stood up. Sitting here feeling sorry for herself and agonising over her possible mistakes wasn't *fixing* anything, was it? It was time to go and find Cristo.

Questioned, Umberto smiled and indicated a door at the foot of a short corridor off the main hall. 'Mr Cristo has been working round the clock in his office since news of the banking crisis broke...'

What banking crisis? Belle had not seen a television or a newspaper since the morning of her wedding. She had noticed that the nanny, Teresa, had a TV in her room but had drawn a blank when she looked for access to one for her own benefit. Perspiration breaking on her brow, she knocked on the door of Cristo's office and then opened it.

Dark eyes flying up from his laptop screen, Cristo swung round in his chair. Belle's appearance shocked him on two levels. *Dio mio,* he had a wife and he had forgotten about her, and then his next thought was that forgetting about her should have been impossible when she was such a beauty, standing in the doorway, a slender, wonderfully leggy figure taut with uncertainty in a peach-coloured top and skirt that toned in perfectly with her torrent of vibrant spiral curls. Wide grass-green eyes assailed his.

'I wondered where you were,' she said awkwardly, transfixed as she always was at first glimpse of his tousled dark head, perfect bronze profile and striking eyes. The fact he hadn't shaved merely added a raw-edged masculinity to his charismatic appeal and she could feel her face warming up, her tummy flipping, her heart rate skipping upbeat: all standard reactions to Cristo. 'Then Umberto mentioned a banking crisis of some kind. I'm afraid I haven't seen a newspaper since I arrived and I didn't know about it. Do you need any help?'

'Help?' Cristo queried, ebony brows rising in surprise. 'How could you help?'

'I have a first-class degree in business and economics and I worked as an intern for a year in a Dublin bank as part of the course,' Belle confided hesitantly.

A line of colour flared across Cristo's cheekbones as it crossed his mind that he should've known such elementary facts about the woman he had married, and rare discomfiture sliced through him. 'I had no idea.'

Her eyes sparkling with genuine amusement, an involuntary grin slanted Belle's wide and generous mouth. 'So, you just assumed you were marrying an uneducated Irish peasant, did you?'

'If you're willing to help, I'd be grateful, *bella mia,*' Cristo admitted, smoothly, gratefully ducking that issue entirely. 'I'm trying to work with my London staff remotely and it's complicated but this is supposed to be our honeymoon.'

'I've got nothing else to do,' Belle pointed

out gently, convinced that a couple of their ilk scarcely qualified for the itinerary or the behaviour of a normal honeymoon couple.

Cristo immediately recognised yet another screaming indictment of his behaviour as a new husband and hurriedly sidestepped that awareness by offering Belle the laptop beside his own and springing upright to ask Umberto to go and find another chair. His conscience reacted as though someone had given it a good hard kick. Marriage, he was learning by slow and painful steps, would demand much more of him than he had imagined and would entail considering Belle's needs as well as his own.

For the first time, he appreciated that he had had absolutely no right to judge his brother, Nik, for the mess he had made of his marriage to Betsy. After all, he only knew *one* side of that story and tiny, fragile Betsy weeping out her heartbreak on Cristo's chest had definitely cornered the sympathy vote as far as appearances went. His lip curled as he skimmed a glance across Belle's composed and lovely face and he almost smiled in relief. There was nothing helpless about Belle and at least she wasn't crying hysterically, complaining, condemning...

'Yes, she's amazing,' Cristo agreed in Italian with his chief finance officer in the London branch of his investment bank. 'If I wasn't married to her, I'd hire her!'

Cristo studied his wife with an involuntary sense of pride. Belle was curled up in a chair with a laptop, long incredible legs in shorts on display, auburn hair spiralling down round her shoulders, enhancing porcelain-pale freckled skin while her fingers flew over the keyboard. It was the pivotal moment when he realised that he had struck literal gold and had seriously underestimated her worth when he married her. For a woman of her beauty to have retained qualities of such natural likeability and unpretentiousness was extraordinary. She was also intelligent, resourceful and hardworking. Not once had she complained over the past three days about the very long hours they were putting in and she had kept pace with him every step of the way. He winced when he recalled the lingerie episode at the fashion show.

Belle stood up to stretch and set the laptop down. The banking crisis was over and she was almost disappointed by that reality since it had acted as a brilliantly positive antidote to the friction between them. They could work together now, talk to each other. He had stopped treating her like some sort of glorified sex doll expected to offer him entertainment and she had learned to her own satisfaction that Cristo was as smart as a whip while being as stubborn and impatient as she was.

Her clear gaze wandered over him while he sprawled back against the edge of the desk, long powerful thighs sheathed in denim splayed, a crisp lemon shirt open at his strong tanned throat. She looked at his wide, sensual lips and recalled the passionate intoxication of his kiss and momentarily felt dizzy. Her mouth ran dry, hunger stirring at the core of her as it had so often in recent days when her body reacted to the presence of his. She leant slightly forward, willing him to make a move to hold her, touch her, kiss her...*anything*!

'Put on something fancy. I'm taking you out to dinner, *bella mia*,' Cristo volunteered, glancing up to transfix her with spectacular dark golden eyes heavily fringed with lush black lashes.

Belle flushed to her hairline, mortified by her thoughts and drawn up short by the unexpected invitation. 'Only if you want to.'

'*Dio mio!* Of course I want to,' Cristo countered with a frown.

'You don't need to thank me for helping out,' Belle told him stubbornly.

Cristo expelled his breath in a slow hiss. 'Is it so hard for you to accept that I might want to take my beautiful wife out and show her off?'

Belle laughed at the idea. 'Not when you put it that way, you smoothie!' she teased.

Cristo winced. 'Don't call me that...it makes me think of Gaetano.'

Belle wrinkled her nose in agreement. 'You don't remind me of him in any way.'

'*Grazie a Dio*...thank God,' Cristo retorted with visible relief.

Belle collided with Franco on the way into the office. Her little brother pushed past her to throw himself at Cristo with a shout of satisfaction. Although they had been incredibly busy in recent days, Cristo never turned Franco away and she appreciated that, glancing back as Cristo tickled Franco and engaged in the kind of rough, noisy, masculine play that the toddler adored. While she hovered, Cristo answered the buzz of his cell phone.

At supersonic speed she registered that something bad had happened and she moved back into the office because Cristo's lean, strong face had clenched into rigid lines, his eyes darkening, his mouth compressing as he finished the call in clipped Italian. He released Franco and the little boy scampered off into the hall, already in search of fresh amusement.

Cristo settled dark eyes now flaming accusing gold on Belle and asked harshly, 'Have you been talking to the press?'

Astonishment furrowed her brow. 'No, of course not! What on earth are you talking about?' she parried, instantly cast on the defensive.

'A friend who's a journalist in London just called me to warn me that the story of Gaetano, your mother and the kids will be appearing in print some time soon in a British tabloid!' Cristo bit out furiously.

Belle paled at that news but rallied fast because her own conscience was clear. 'Well, that's very unfortunate.'

Cristo sprang upright, six feet plus inches of enraged, darkly powerful masculinity. *'Unfortunate?* Is that all you think this is?'

Infuriated by his attitude and wounded by the speed with which he had leapt to distrust, Belle squared her slight shoulders against the wall, her lovely face flushed and taut with strain. 'Keep this in proportion, Cristo, and try to be reasonable.'

'Reasonable?' he growled as if he didn't rec-

ognise the word. 'I married you to keep that sleazy story out of the newspapers!'

And just then, Belle could have done without the reminder of that fact.

'I always thought it was unlikely that you could prevent that story from *ever* coming out,' she admitted reluctantly. 'My mum was with your father for almost twenty years and everyone for miles around, who enjoyed a bit of gossip, knew about their relationship and the children. All it would have taken was for *one* person to talk to the wrong person, who saw some chance of profit in the information and the secret would have emerged.'

Lean tanned hands clenching into fists by his side, Cristo jerked his arrogant dark head in grudging acknowledgement of that possibility, his innate intelligence warring with his equally natural aggressive instincts to persuade him that she was talking sense.

Belle prowled forward like a stalking tigress and flicked his shirtfront with an angry finger. 'But how dare you even *think* that it might have been me who leaked the story to the press?' she launched at him, green eyes bright with indignation. 'I wouldn't do that to my brothers and sisters. They've already paid a high enough price for the sins of their parents and the very last thing I would ever want to do is upset them more!'

'I didn't accuse you.'

'You *asked* me if I had been talking to the press. What sort of a question was that to ask your wife? What reason would I have to expose all of us to that kind of unpleasant public attention?' Belle demanded.

'Revenge? Gaetano may be dead but you hate his guts and never got the chance to tell him so. In fact I suspect you distrust and dislike anyone called Ravelli!' Cristo slammed back at her in condemnation.

'I've changed.' Yet Belle wanted so badly to slap him that her palm tingled. Only the knowledge that *before* she met him she had had that attitude burned her deep with shame, for one thing she had learned to appreciate since then was that Gaetano's hedonistic lifestyle had damaged almost every life he touched, not least those of the children he had fathered without parenting. 'Well, then I'd have a real problem with my identity, wouldn't I?' she fired back with ringing disdain. 'Considering that now I'm a Ravelli too.'

'*Sì,* and my wife, *cara mia.*' Cristo found himself suddenly savouring that reality as he looked at her, aggression switching into another similarly testosterone-driven reaction, his attention surging from her beautiful defiant face down to her heaving breasts shimmying below the light tee she wore, arousal roaring through him like an engine revving up.

'But not so happy to be your wife right now!' Belle hissed a split second before Cristo cornered her by the wall, closing an ensnaring hand into her tumbling curls to tip up her mouth and then silencing any objection she might have made with the heat of his own.

Belle pushed against his chest but it was, at most, a half-hearted protest because, as fired up by emotion as she was, she couldn't fight the overwhelming rush of sexual hunger that assailed her the instant Cristo touched her. His kisses were ravenous, both of his hands fisted in her hair, his lean, powerful body pinning her to the wall while his tongue teased and delved inside her mouth with ravishing force. A moan was wrenched from her lips as he squeezed the straining bud of one tender nipple through her clothing and the sensation ran like dynamite to the aching heart of her. She felt frantic, possessed, needy way beyond anything she had ever experienced before.

Belle wrenched at his shirt, struggling with the buttons and then finally yanking in frustration at the barrier between them, so that the buttons flew and the shirt parted and he drew back for an instant. She was shocked by what she had done, her colour high but, regardless, she succumbed to the overpowering desire to mould her palms to the hard planes of his hair-roughened chest and feel the wild heat and strength of his very masculine body.

'I've never wanted any woman as much as I want you,' Cristo bit out, taking a long stride away from her to slam the door shut, turn the lock and stalk back to her with clear devastating intent in his devouring gaze.

And Belle had never known what hunger felt like until she met him and, even though she was shaken by her own primitive urges, her passionate desire was stoked higher by the boldly visible erection he sported below his chinos. 'Take off the shirt,' she told him.

'Getting bossy now?' Cristo quipped as he dropped it on the floor.

'Oh, you have no idea,' she murmured, relishing the sight of his powerfully muscled chest and impressive abs, helpless anticipation lancing through her as she curled her fingers into his belt and hauled him back to her.

At that point, Cristo flung back his handsome dark head and laughed, lowering his head to kiss her again in the midst of lifting her silk top up and up and finally, somewhat clumsily for a man of his sophistication, off over her head.

She was not wearing a bra and he shaped the firm full globes he had revealed with reverent hands, thumbs and fingers stroking over the swollen tips. 'I *love* your curves,' he confided with husky emphasis, skating his palms down admiringly over the sloping softness of her hips before his hand slid below the skirt and ran unerringly up the hot skin of her inner thigh. Lost in the grip of urgent need, she angled away from the wall towards him, wanting, inviting, and truly *needing* his touch.

Her eyes slid shut as he teased the swollen hot flesh already damp with desire at the heart of her and, with a little sound of impatience, he knelt down to dispose of her panties and lingered to appreciate that most tender part of her with his tongue and his sensually skilled mouth.

'Cristo!' Belle gasped.

'For the last three nights while you went to your bed and I went to mine, I've been dreaming about doing this,' Cristo confessed with carnal boldness, the low growl of his roughened intonation vibrating down her spine.

He tasted her and savoured her as though she were the finest wine and intoxicating waves of sensation engulfed Belle until she was trembling and only the wall and his arm at her hips were keeping her upright against that seductive onslaught. Only when she literally couldn't take any more of the taunting, delirious pleasure that he wouldn't allow to progress to its natural conclusion did he sweep her up in his arms and sit her down on the edge of the desk. Once she was in position, he stepped between her spread thighs and crushed her reddened mouth below his again with a primal insistence that consumed her like an adrenalin shot injected straight into her veins.

'I didn't see us doing this…*here*,' Belle muttered shakily.

'I don't know how I kept my hands off you the last few days, *bellezza mia*,' Cristo confided hoarsely, nuzzling his cheek down the extended length of her throat with a deeply expressive masculine groan of agreement. 'I didn't want to rock the boat.'

'Rock it!' Belle urged him on breathlessly as he began to push inside her, her inner walls initially protesting the unflinching demand of his entrance and then slowly stretching around him with a delicious sensation of fullness that made her moan in elated response.

His hands firm on her hips, Cristo tipped her back and then he drove home to the hilt with a power and immediacy that was even more thrilling for her highly aroused body. He pulled back and then slammed home again, jolting her with an excitement that ran like a river of fire through every erogenous zone she possessed. Her heart was racing, her entire body straining and pleading for the ultimate climax while he increased the speed of his strokes, driving faster, deeper while the frenzy of her need and exhilaration combined into a wild rollercoaster ride of ever-increasing pleasure. Her body clenched and she convulsed, crying out and quivering as the pleasure burst like shooting fireworks inside her, sending surge after surge of breathtaking ecstasy travelling through her trembling body.

Cristo wasn't quite sure he could stay upright as his own climax engulfed him and he held her close, groaning out loud as he spilled his seed inside her, and the very newness of that sensation sent him back on full alert. '*Che diavolo!*' he exclaimed in consternation, immediately imagining the worst possible scenario. 'I didn't use a condom!'

Taken aback by the sudden admission, Belle blinked uncertainly as he wrapped both arms round her and steadied them both. 'Oh…' she framed against his chest, his heart thundering against her cheek, the musky male scent of his skin wonderfully familiar and extraordinarily soothing to her now.

'I've never ever *not* used one before,' Cristo assured her in a driven undertone. 'You got me so worked up.'

'It's all right,' she mumbled, hiding a smile of satisfaction at the awareness that she could be responsible for exciting him to the extent that he failed to exercise his usual self-discipline. 'I started taking the pill before the wedding, so there shouldn't be any consequences.'

Cristo pictured Franco purely in terms of a consequence and was quite astounded to recognise the tiniest pang of disappointment when she reassured him that there was no risk of such a development. He shook his handsome dark head as if to clear it of such an insane thought, seriously rattled by it and where it might have come from. He had no desire for a child, had never had a desire for one and yet there was something about Franco...

'You're incredible, *bellezza mia*,' he husked, blanking out those unsettling weird reflections in favour of kissing her brow, the tip of her nose and finally her luscious mouth. 'You have a passion and an ability to excite me that most men can only dream about finding with one woman.'

Slowly, carefully he lowered her back down to the floor before helpfully lifting her top to slide over her head and back over her torso. Dazed, she leant back against the desk again, cheeks as hot as coals, eyes screened by her lashes as she absorbed that last statement with pleasure but also because she was shockingly disconcerted by the wildness they had shared and the sheer screaming intimacy of the experience.

A couple of hours later and groomed to within an inch of her life, those tumultuous emotions and sensations carefully tamped down, Belle scrutinised her reflection with a sharply critical gaze. It was a beautiful dress and her youngest sister would have told her that she looked like a princess in it because Lucia, in common with their late mother, adored feminine frills. Pale pink and full length, the gown was bare at the shoulder and moulded to her figure at breast and hip. Did she look just a little *too* busty? She hitched the bodice and then almost laughed, pretty much convinced when she thought about it that Cristo would enjoy the view.

Betsy rang Cristo as he emerged from the shower in his own room next door. He listened as he always did but he felt strangely detached from his sister-in-law and her problems. It occurred to him that he had never lusted after Nik's wife the way he did after his own and he marvelled at that reality, wondering if some internal censor button had somehow prevented it or whether indeed she didn't appeal to him quite that much on that more basic level, which struck him as an extraordinary possibility.

He was *still* listening to Betsy recount the latest hostile moves his brother had made in the divorce battle when Belle came downstairs and his mind went totally blank because Belle looked fantastic and he couldn't think of anything else. He ended the call with an apologetic mutter.

'Who were you talking to?' Belle asked, her attention locked to the unusually distracted expression on his lean dark features.

'Betsy.'

'Nik's wife?'

Cristo struggled not to sound defensive. 'We're friends.'

'That must be awkward,' Belle remarked. 'Were you friends before they got married?'

Cristo tensed, a muscle pulling taut at the corner of his shapely mouth. 'No. It happened because of the way they broke up.'

Like a bloodhound on the trail, Belle was in no mood to settle for less than she wanted to know. 'And why *did* they break up?'

'For very private reasons. But something I let slip when I should have kept quiet and minded my own business contributed to it.' Cristo framed that admission of guilt in a harsh undertone. 'I'm sorry I can't tell you more but I caused a lot of trouble by once carelessly revealing a secret which Nik had shared with me and…I definitely have lived to regret it.'

Belle wanted to drag the whole truth out of him there and then because all her suspicious antennae were now waking up to full alert. Exactly what did his 'friendship' with Betsy Ravelli entail?

Outside the limousine awaited them. 'Where are we going?' she asked to fill the strained silence, which confirmed for her that there had to be a very good reason why Cristo was quite so wary and uncomfortable when it came to discussing his brother's estranged wife. Was she being fanciful in being so suspicious? *Was* his reaction simply the result of his guilty conviction that he might have contributed to the breakdown of the couple's marriage? But if that was true, why did he carry a photo of Betsy in his wallet? That lent an all too personal dimension to the relationship that could only make Belle feel troubled.

'We're going to Assisi. There's a very special restaurant there,' Cristo imparted, relieved she had dropped the touchy subject of Nik's marriage breakdown.

'Assisi…as in the birthplace of St Francis?'

Cristo gave her a droll look. 'There is only one.'

'To be actually going there just feels so weird. It was my mother's lifelong dream to visit Assisi. She was a great believer in the power of St Francis,' Belle explained, a certain amount of embarrassment at that unsophisticated admission mingling with the very real sadness that claimed her when something touched on her many memories of the older woman.

'And Gaetano never brought Mary to Italy?' Cristo prompted in surprise.

'Are you kidding? He never took Mum anywhere,' Belle countered between compressed lips of grim recollection. 'Their relationship only existed behind closed doors.'

'And your mother didn't object to that?'

'No and what's more she *still* thought the sun rose and fell on him. Gaetano didn't take her money, knock her around or get drunk, so in her opinion he was perfection. She wasn't very bright or well educated,' Belle proffered in a guilty undertone because she felt disloyal making that statement about the parent she had loved. 'But she was a very loving, loyal and kind person.'

'She must also have been very tolerant and forgiving. That's probably why their affair lasted so long,' Cristo commented with a wry twist of his mouth.

Belle's throat thickened with tears and she

swallowed with difficulty. 'Sometimes I miss her so much it *hurts*,' she admitted quietly.

Cristo tensed when he noticed the glimmer of moisture on her cheeks. He breathed in slow and deep, unfroze his big powerful body with difficulty and pushed himself to close a hand over her tightly clenched fingers where they rested on her lap. 'I can't even say that I can imagine how you feel because it would be a lie,' he conceded ruefully. 'I'm not particularly close to my mother and I had no relationship with Gaetano to mourn when he died. You're fortunate to be a part of such a close family.'

In silence, Belle nestled her fingers beneath the warmth of his and marvelled at that unexpectedly thoughtful gesture of comfort and the sentiment from his corner.

They dined at a table set for two on a massive terrace surrounded by amazing views of the picturesque hillside town. The streets they had driven through had been a geranium-hung blaze of flowering colour and she had caught glimpses of medieval back lanes and piazzas adorned with ancient fountains.

'Where are all the other customers?' Belle asked, surveying the empty tables around them.

'Tonight, we're the *only* customers and one of Italy's most famous chefs is cooking solely for us, *bella mia*.'

'And you arranged it that way?' Belle prompted in amazement.

'This is the very first time I've taken you anywhere,' Cristo pointed out bluntly. 'And we've been married a week, which basically tells me that I owe you a decent night out. I also owe you for all the work you put in for me without complaint.'

'I like working. I like feeling useful,' Belle confessed truthfully, green eyes sparkling, generous mouth warming into an unrestrained smile because simply sitting there in her beautiful dress with her even more beautiful husband opposite made her feel ridiculously spoilt and contented.

Hungry desire flaming through him afresh

and coalescing in an ache of raw need so eager to stir at his groin, Cristo studied his wife, marvelling at the explosive effect she had on his libido. Although he didn't consider himself to be either an emotional or sentimental man, he found her natural warmth and liveliness amazingly attractive.

The waiter brought the menu and the chef came out to greet them and offer recommendations. By then dusk was falling and the candles were lit. Belle cradled her wine and sipped, rejoicing in the fact that she could at last relax in Cristo's company.

'You still haven't explained why Bruno and Donetta were sent to boarding school,' Cristo drawled lazily.

Her fingers tightened round the glass in her hand. 'Bruno was never an athletic boy and he finally admitted to Gaetano that he was only interested in art. Your father asked him if he was gay…he was only thirteen at the time,' she completed in a tone of disgust.

Cristo swore under his breath.

'Then Gaetano decided to make that a running joke and whenever he saw Bruno after that he called him "gay boy". Eventually someone else overheard and talked and Bruno started getting bullied at school but he didn't tell us what was happening,' Belle explained heavily, having to pause to breathe in deep before she could continue to tell the distressing truth. 'Bruno tried to kill himself but, very fortunately for us and him, we found him in time and he recovered.'

Cristo was honestly appalled by the confession while he recalled that skinny-wristed boy with the anxious eyes who had cornered him on the day of the wedding. 'I was remarkably lucky, it seems, to escape Gaetano's concept of how to be a good father.'

'Well, after that Donetta finally picked up the courage to tell us what had been going on at school and that's why they both went into boarding,' Belle advanced. 'Bruno's experience with Gaetano is the main reason why I hated your father. And my brother, by the way, is *not* gay.'

'It wouldn't have made any difference to me if

he was,' Cristo remarked as the first course was deferentially laid before them. 'The poor kid.'

'He's a very talented artist and the change of environment was exactly what he needed, even if it does mean he and Donetta are separated from the family.'

'When they move to London, they won't be separated any longer,' Cristo reminded her. 'They can attend a day school or even board and come home at weekends—whichever they would prefer... It's up to them.'

'I know. I wanted us all to be together again,' she confided ruefully. 'But you might find it a little crowded with all of us around.'

Cristo dealt her a wicked look teeming with all the passion that simmered so close to the surface of his apparently controlled exterior. 'I think I will enjoy being crowded by you.'

CHAPTER NINE

WITH A GROWING sense of awe, Belle studied the laptop pictures of the latest London property details sent for their perusal by the consultant hired by Cristo. Cristo had told Belle simply to pick a house, as his penthouse apartment was too small to house her family. He had very little interest in what his new home would be like, having merely specified a room to house an office and sufficient space in which to entertain. Belle was staggered, not only by the sheer meteoric cost and superb appointments of the elite properties tendered to them, but also by the level of responsibility Cristo had entrusted her with.

At the same time, she would have been the first to admit that during the past weeks in Italy their relationship had changed out of all recognition. Most mornings she helped Cristo catch up in the office. After that they would spend the rest of the day exploring, eating out, swimming, generally just relaxing and often with Franco in tow. And equally often they would sit out until very late talking over guttering candles on the terrace where they usually dined. A dreamy expression clouded Belle's eyes in tune with the increasing sense of security that she was feeling in her new life. Nothing seemed that daunting with Cristo by her side. No, not even his mother, Princess Giulia, who had arrived with his stepfather, Henri Montaldo, with very little warning only the day before. Belle's mother-in-law had literally shrieked in infuriated horror once she finally grasped the identity of the woman whom her one and only child had married.

'What are the children of this unscrupulous Irish woman to do with you?' the princess, an imperious, ageless little brunette dressed in the latest fashion, had demanded in outrage of her son.

'They are my family,' Cristo had responded quietly and Belle's chest had swelled with pride, for she knew what an achievement it was that he had now moved beyond his original feelings to regard her siblings in that just and unselfish light.

And the battle between mother and son had then switched to incomprehensible volleys of furious Italian while Belle offered Cristo's step-father, Henri, a mild-mannered man, coffee and tried to pretend that she wasn't aware that his wife was undoubtedly engaged in attacking Belle's late parent, Mary, for the reckless choices she had made in life.

'Gaetano is Giulia's one blind spot,' Henri had remarked ruefully under cover of the argument raging back and forth between mother and son. 'He was the love of her life.'

'Yet you've been together…?' Belle had begun awkwardly.

'Since Cristo was a toddler,' Henri had confirmed in the same even, accepting manner. 'Don't worry about this. Cristo will settle it. He knows how to handle his mother.'

By the time the coffee was being served, the

argument had become a much less tense discussion laced with Henri's soothing comments, and Belle swiftly recognised that Cristo both liked and respected his stepfather. Indeed by the time the volatile princess had departed, the older woman had recovered her mood to the extent of ruffling Franco's black curly hair, remarking what a very handsome little boy he was and kissing Belle on both cheeks and welcoming her to the family. The threat of lingering bad feelings that Belle had feared might result from such an encounter had been successfully averted.

'So, as you witnessed this afternoon, everybody gets embarrassed when it comes to family members,' Cristo had remarked in bed the night before while she still lay boneless and weak with drowning contentment in the circle of his arms. 'My mother has a very short fuse. She loses her head and throws scenes.'

'But she calms back down again and she doesn't hold spite,' Belle pointed out lightly. 'That's a plus.'

'I didn't want her to upset you, *bellezza mia*,' Cristo admitted. 'It's more than a quarter of a century since she divorced Gaetano and, let's face it, what he did after that and who he did it with is none of her business.'

'But at one time she obviously cared a lot for him,' Belle mused, drowsily settling her head down on his smooth bronzed shoulder, breathing in the scent of him in a state of sublime relaxation. 'And his infidelity and his lies must have hurt her enormously. A woman would've needed to be hard as a rock or wilfully blind like my mother to handle Gaetano without getting chewed up into little pieces.'

'I'll always be honest with you,' Cristo declared, long tanned fingers skimming her tousled curls back from her brow as he looked down at her, dark eyes sexy gold below the stunning black of his luxuriant lashes. 'I can promise you that much.'

That was a big promise and an even bigger temptation, Belle reflected sleepily. She knew she ought to ask him about the photo in his wallet but just at that moment when she felt deliciously happy and comfortable felt like the wrong moment and she kicked the idea back out of her head with relief. No man had ever made her feel secure the way Cristo did, she conceded blissfully. She would ask him some time soon and would no doubt quickly learn that she had been agonising over nothing. Perhaps he had had the photo for some reason and had simply forgotten he still had it...

Recalling that thought, Belle drifted back to the present to find Cristo on the pool terrace regarding her where she reclined in the shade with an abandoned book, his amusement unhidden. 'You were a thousand miles away.'

'So, I daydream sometimes,' Belle parried, studying him with helpless appreciation: a lithe sun-bronzed god of a male, lean, powerful frame garbed in black jeans and a white tee. His breathtaking good looks still enthralled her but then *she* wasn't the only one looking, she recognised with pleasure as Cristo's gaze whipped with flattering appreciation over her bikini-clad curves. 'Were you looking for me?'

'*Sì.*' Cristo hesitated. 'I'm flying the rest of your family here this afternoon.'

Brow furrowed in surprise, Belle sat up. 'What are you talking about?'

'I've been warned that the story about Gaetano and his children by your mother will be published tomorrow, so I'm taking your grandmother and the children out of harm's way and over here where no one will bother them.'

Thrown off balance by that terse explanation, Belle exclaimed, 'When did you decide to do that? My gran as well? They won't want to come at such short notice, for goodness' sake.'

'Bruno's bored stiff at home over the summer and counting the hours. I Skyped him and he believes he will like the Umbrian landscape,' Cristo supplied with a decided hint of one-upmanship.

'You *Skyped* him?' Belle gasped in complete disconcertion.

'I alerted your grandmother to the situation

last week. She's now only awaiting your call to reassure her that they won't be intruding on us,' Cristo completed.

'But she never said a word when I last spoke to her...' Belle's voice trailed away, for she could scarcely recall what she had discussed with the older woman during that call and would have been the first to admit that her concentration hadn't been what it was of late. More and more her entire world seemed to be defined by the closed little world she inhabited with Cristo, where nothing else seemed to matter very much.

'She didn't want to worry you, so will you ring her and assure her they're all welcome and that we have plenty of space for them?' Cristo prompted. 'The experience of having the paparazzi on the doorstep would be traumatic for the children.'

Pale and dismayed at the threat of her family being exposed to that kind of rude and humiliating attention, Belle was propelled straight off the lounger and back indoors.

When she phoned her grandmother, Isa was

her usual calm and logical self. 'Whatever happens we'll weather it the way we've weathered everything else. You don't *have* to bring us to Italy,' she declared staunchly.

'I'm dying to see you all again. I know it's only been a few weeks but it feels more like months,' Belle confided truthfully. 'And Franco keeps on asking for you all.'

'Newly married couples need privacy and five children and a granny are going to put quite a dent in that,' Isa forecast ruefully.

'You're family—that's different,' Belle protested. 'And I've missed you all so much.'

And that was true, regardless of her contentment with Cristo, she acknowledged. In fact her time away from the family had already taught her how much she had taken their presence for granted before her marriage and how much she had since missed the warm hurly-burly of their home and her grandmother's soothing support.

With her family's coming visit confirmed, Belle went off to consult Umberto about where everyone was to sleep and discovered that

Cristo had already spoken to him on the subject the week before. Isa suffered from arthritic knees and sometimes found stairs a challenge and Belle was further disconcerted to learn that a room downstairs that opened out on a seating area on the terrace had already been set up for the older woman's occupation.

'When did you organise the room for Isa?' Belle asked Cristo curiously as she came to a halt in the doorway of his office.

'As soon as I knew she was coming, *bellezza mia*. My grandmother also preferred ground-floor accommodation,' Cristo told her quietly.

Belle collided with his spectacular dark heavily fringed eyes and her heart hammered behind her breastbone. 'Is your grandmother still alive?'

'No. She died the summer after I graduated but she was very much a part of my life when I was younger,' Cristo admitted.

'How does your brother Zarif feel about the news article that's about to be published?' Belle asked worriedly. 'I know how worried you were about the effect it might have on him.'

'Zarif never panics and he believes that such a juicy story was always going to escape into the public domain. He says he'll ride it out.'

In receipt of that assurance, Belle felt a little of her tension evaporate. She wanted to ask Cristo if he now felt that he had married her for nothing. After all, he had married her to bury that story and the safeguard hadn't worked. 'That's good.'

Cristo sprang upright, his attention pinned to Belle's pensive face, the sparkle in her eyes and the ripe curve of her mouth. 'You're happy your family's coming to stay, aren't you?'

Belle cast off her insecurities and a grin relaxed her mouth. 'Yes. I've missed them a lot.'

'I really didn't appreciate how close you all were. Growing up, I was strictly an only child. I first met my half-brothers when I was a teenager and only then because my stepfather argued in favour of it.'

Within hours, Cristo received an emailed

copy of the article that was to be published in a leading tabloid newspaper the following day.

'You've been immortalised in print!' Cristo growled from the doorway of the bedroom where Belle was putting a pile of fashion magazines in place for her younger sister, Lucia. A dark flush had overlaid his hard cheekbones and his eyes were bright with anger.

Belle whirled round to study him the instant she glimpsed the papers that he was angrily burnishing. 'I beg your pardon?'

Her heart in her mouth, she stared down at the email he'd printed out, spread flat on the table beside her. The headline *'Ravelli's Secret Irish Family'* spelt out the facts and shock reverberated through Belle when she saw the number of photos in the spread, not least the one of her clad in her wedding gown, which looked rather as though it might have been taken by a camera phone outside the chapel on the day. The main picture, however, was of her pregnant mother and her siblings taken at a local fair shortly before Franco's birth. There was even a small snap of her grandmother.

'So, the story really is going to be printed... I'm so sorry. I know how you felt about this,' Belle breathed heavily.

'But how *dare* they publish a photo of you?' Cristo demanded in a raw undertone, stabbing the offending item with a blunt forefinger. 'Smearing you with Gaetano's sleaze as if *you* had anything to do with your mother's choices!'

Disconcerted by the focus of his rage, Belle swallowed hard. 'Who was it who talked to the press?'

'Gaetano's former driver.'

Belle was hurriedly reading the article, noting with relief that her grandmother was referred to as 'well-respected' and that she was merely mentioned as Mary's 'recently married' daughter. 'Luckily nobody seems to have made the connection that I got married to a Ravelli,' she remarked in astonishment. 'In fact there's no reference to you at all—'

'Isn't there?' Frowning in surprise at that

news, Cristo bent to scan the blurred newsprint. 'Well, that's something at least.'

'And it doesn't say anything that isn't true. I mean, Gaetano *was* married throughout most of their affair and my mother wasn't the only woman in his life at the time.' Belle breathed in deep, colliding head-on with his burnished gaze and feeling her tummy flip in response. 'You know, I think the article could have been a lot nastier in tone than this is.'

'I just don't like you being soiled with Gaetano's sleaze,' Cristo admitted in a roughened undertone while he ran an admiring finger along the softened line of her generous mouth. 'But I suppose you're right and if Zarif can handle the fallout, we certainly can.'

Almost of their own volition her lips parted and she laved his fingertip with the tip of her tongue. His lashes lowered, his semi-screened eyes flashing burning gold and scorchingly light against his bronzed skin as he hauled her into his arms and covered her mouth hungrily with his own. Excitement flared through Belle's slender body like a storm warning and the instant surge of desire stirred a sharp ache between her thighs.

'I want you,' Cristo ground out against her swollen lips, arching her into him with an imprisoning hand splayed across her hips, ensuring that she was fully aware of his arousal.

Belle lifted an unsteady hand to his lean dark face and her fingertips traced a hard masculine cheekbone in a helpless caress. 'Well, I'm not doing anything else...' she whispered teasingly, hot as an inferno inside her own skin and literally weak with longing.

He took that invitation with a thoroughness she could only appreciate. Lifting her in his arms, he took her back to their bedroom. Her heated bare skin revelled in the brush of the cool, crisp linen on the bed when he tossed the sheets back. She was excited by the crushing weight of her lover and his forcefulness as he stretched her arms above her head, her wrists gripped between the fingers of one strong hand, and ravished her mouth erotically with his own.

Between the sheets, Cristo was dominant and she rejoiced in that aspect of him. Her heart thundered in her ears as he stroked and teased the tender tissue between her thighs, her slender spine arching in helpless delight as he took advantage of the welcome offered by the honeyed dampness of her sensitive flesh.

When Cristo flipped her over onto her knees, a sound of surprise was wrenched from her and then, before she could say or do anything, he was driving into her hard and fast, stretching her with shocking fullness, every entry and withdrawal perfectly timed to deliver the maximum possible pleasure. Insane excitement roared through Belle like a hungry fire, burning up every thought in the heat of the flames. She was out of control, lost in sensation, a slave to the delight. Her body raced to the climax it craved and she cried out in pure ecstasy, hearing his answering groan. Afterwards she collapsed in a heap on the bed, her muscles like jelly, her breath still hissing in and out of her gasping throat as she struggled to reason and speak again.

'Did I ever tell you how fantastic you are in bed, *bella mia*?' Cristo husked, pulling her back against his hard, damp body, his broad chest still heaving from the exertion of their encounter.

'Maybe you've mentioned it once or twice.' A smile as old as Eve curved Belle's reddened mouth because it made her feel good that he could think that even in the light of his much greater sexual experience.

Black hair wildly tousled, Cristo rubbed a stubbled jaw across a slim, smooth shoulder and murmured earthily, 'I can't keep my hands off you...you're killing me.'

Belle laughed softly and curved round him, every possessive urge in her body thrumming on full charge. She was happy, so happy that the horrible newspaper article hadn't rocked their relationship as she'd once feared, but still a sense of unease niggled in the back of her mind. The moment she looked for it, that tiny little seed of doubt about Cristo and Betsy refused to stay buried any longer. She wanted, no, she *needed* to know the truth, which she was convinced would be entirely non-threatening in reality.

'Why do you carry a photo of your brother's wife in your wallet?' Belle lifted her head to ask, the question as bold and instinctive on her lips as it was in her mind.

CHAPTER TEN

CRISTO'S BIG, POWERFUL frame froze and, that fast, Belle knew she had made a fatal mistake in assuming that she had nothing to worry about.

Dark blood rose in a revealing banner across Cristo's cheekbones. His spectacular bone structure had hardened into taut angles and hollows overlaid with the rigidity of fierce self-control while his dark golden eyes remained carefully shielded. 'What are you talking about?'

No longer warm and relaxed in the intimate circle of his arms, Belle rolled away and sat up against the tumbled pillows, tugging the sheet up to cover her breasts with hands that now felt clumsy. 'Franco got hold of your wallet one day and the photo fell out of it. I wasn't snooping, I *swear* I wasn't, but naturally I wondered why you had it.'

'Franco,' Cristo groaned, raking the long fingers of one tanned hand through his black hair and sitting up while he played for time and considered his options. That blasted photo, which he had forgotten he still had! He could lie, of course he could lie to her, but the memory of Gaetano's frequent lies and deceptions had left his son with an ineradicable desire never to follow in the older man's footsteps. Besides, lying was not only a weakness but also an act of deceit. Belle was his wife and she was entitled to the truth, he reasoned grimly, even if it was a truth he was in no hurry to share or recall. But where there was honesty, he believed there would be no future misunderstandings or grey areas.

He breathed in deep and slow and then released his breath again in an impatient hiss, his handsome mouth compressing. 'Betsy turned to me for support after her marriage to Nik broke down...for a while I thought I'd fallen in love with her...'

Belle was already in the grip of mental turmoil because his visible reaction to her question had immediately betrayed that she had stumbled onto a sensitive issue. Her head ached with the ferocity of her tension and her conflicting thoughts and incipient panic made her a poor listener. *I fell in love with her* was all Belle took from that fractured speech and his confession had the same impact on her as the announcement of a sudden death. *I fell for her.* Her mouth ran dry, her heartbeat accelerated and her tummy performed a sick somersault. *I fell for her.* She could feel the blood draining from her face, the clawing clench of her fingertips on the edge of the sheet and the resulting ache in her knuckle bones. For a truly dreadful moment she was scared she might throw up where she sat, and then mercifully the tide of sickness receded while her brain kicked feverishly back into action.

Cristo had fallen in love with little fairy-like Betsy, who was so tiny and exquisite that Belle was convinced that she herself would look like a comic-book character standing beside her. Belle was taller, curvier, and physically larger in every way, her hair raucous red to Betsy's pale, subtle blonde. No two women could have been more diametrically opposed in the looks department. Did he try to fantasise that she was Betsy in bed? That cruel suspicion pierced Belle like a knife in her chest, shock still winging through her in blinding waves while her mind leapt on to make even more offensive connections. Cristo had actually dared to marry her when he was in love with another woman! Appalled at this knowledge that sucked out every atom of her former happiness and contentment in her role, Belle slid out of bed and swept up her wrap. She folded herself into it in a jerky motion because her limbs still felt oddly detached from her body.

'Why on earth did you marry *me*?' Anger was roaring through Belle in a giant floodtide that drowned every rational thought and controlled every response. 'I mean, you were in love with another woman, so why the heck would you ask me to marry you?'

Taken aback by her behaviour, his incomprehension growing at her overreaction to what he now saw as a comparatively insignificant mistake on his own part that had caused no one any harm, Cristo frowned in bewilderment. 'Why should it bother you?'

'It doesn't bother me. I'm not one bit bothered!' Belle proclaimed in furious vehement denial, her pride answering for her. 'But obviously I don't like what it says about *you*. What sort of man gets involved with his brother's wife?'

Understanding crossed Cristo's sleek dark face, swiftly followed by an unmistakeable expression of distaste. 'I wasn't sexually involved with Betsy. I didn't make a single move that crossed the boundaries of friendship with her.'

'Are you trying to tell me that you *haven't* had an affair with her?' Belle demanded incredulously. 'Do I look that stupid?'

Honesty, it suddenly struck Cristo for the first time, could be a poisoned chalice. His gift of honesty, offered with the best of intentions, had simply stirred up more serious suspicions. He sprang out of bed and reached for his jeans, pulling them on commando style in a fluid motion. Stunning dark eyes met unflinchingly with Belle's accusing stare.

'There was never any question of an affair. For a start, I never told Betsy how I felt, and naturally there was no physical intimacy. *Dio mio*, she's my brother's wife. I couldn't possibly cross that line.'

'But they're getting a divorce!' Belle cut in furiously.

'Nik will always be my brother. I could still *never* go there and from the outset I accepted that there was no future in my feelings for her.'

'Yet you married me even though you *loved* her!' Belle reminded him painfully, scarcely able to frame the words through her chattering teeth. She felt cold and clammy and nauseous. She had never felt so hurt and rejected in her entire life and it was as though a great well of anguish deep inside her was threatening to drag her down and swallow her alive. Suddenly the world looked dark, her future empty and full of threat.

'Why shouldn't I have married you? How I believed I felt about Betsy is pretty much irrelevant now. There was no way I was ever going to have anything but a friendship with her, and let's not forget that you and I agreed to a marriage purely based on practicality.'

That reminder was brutally unwelcome. Belle's nails bit painfully into the flesh of her hands as she knotted them together. A *practical* marriage. When had she contrived to forget that revealing description of his expectations and her own agreement on that basis? When had she developed expectations of something a great deal more emotionally satisfying than a detached marriage of convenience? And whatever the answer to those questions was it didn't really matter at a moment when she was in so much pain that she could barely bring herself to look at him. Just then she was too worked up to argue with Cristo and she was desperate to make an escape lest she embarrass herself by saying something she shouldn't.

'Excuse me,' Belle breathed curtly, sidestepping Cristo to stalk into the bathroom.

The door closed, the lock turning with a fast and audible click.

In frustration, Cristo swore under his breath. Why was she so angry? Why the hell was she so angry with him? Blasted relationships, he reflected with brooding resentment. He was no good at them, and never had been. He had always settled for sex and got out before anything more complex was required. But he couldn't walk away from Belle and their marriage any more easily than he could escape the fallout from what appeared to be a disastrous error of judgement on his part. He pictured Belle's face when he had truthfully answered her question. She had turned pale as snow, her eyes blank while immediate constraint tightened her features. One minute she had been in his arms, smiling and happy and affectionate, the next angry and distant and...*hurt*. His wide sensual mouth compressed grimly at that awareness. Every natural instinct told him he should have lied in his teeth and made up an excuse for still having that photo in his wallet.

But although he had told her about Betsy, it had decidedly not been the moment to tell her the rest of that story because she would never have believed him in the mood she was in, he reasoned bitterly.

Trembling with reaction, Belle splashed her face with cold water. Tears were running from her eyes and she washed them away with punitive splashes of more cold water, finally burying her chilled face with a shudder in a soft warm towel. Cristo was in love with Betsy and nothing had ever hurt Belle so much as that discovery. Why was that? she asked herself wretchedly; why was she taking the news so badly, so...*personally*?

They had married for convenience and her main motivation before the wedding had been the welfare of her brothers and sisters. That goal had been achieved most successfully for Cristo was already accepting that her siblings were also his and therefore family to them both. He wasn't going to turn round and suddenly desert the children, he was too honourable for that, she reflected heavily. To date he had also kept his promises to her. To say the very least, he treated her with warmth and respect.

Had she hoped he felt more than that where she was concerned? Belle nibbled at her lower lip, afraid to meet her own eyes in the mirror because, on her terms, their relationship had very quickly become intensely personal both in and out of bed. The limits of practicality had been bypassed and forgotten by her within days of the wedding. She had learned to care for Cristo, to enjoy his company, his sense of humour, his kindness to Franco, his thought-fulness whenever it came to a question of what made her happy. In short she had travelled all the way from initial admiration and apprecia-tion to falling madly in love with her husband, which was why hearing that he loved some-one else had caused her such pain. Stupid, *stupid* man—why on earth had he told her? And, even worse, why had he looked at her as though she was insane when she reacted with furious condemnation? Didn't he understand *anything* about women? About her? Maybe she should have framed the experience in terms he would have understood...

'Cristo!' Belle bawled across the bedroom on her noisy return, the bathroom door still shuddering behind her from her aggressive exit.

Cristo emerged from the dressing room in the act of buttoning a shirt and fixed enquiring dark eyes on her with exaggerated politeness. 'You called, *bella mia*?'

Belle reddened fiercely. 'All right, I shouted. I'm sorry. It's just you don't seem to understand how I feel, so I thought I should give you an example.'

A winged ebony brow elevated. 'An example?'

'Try to imagine how you would feel if I was to tell you right now that I was in love with Mark Petrie,' she urged.

Before her very eyes, Cristo froze into an icy bronzed statue. *'Are* you?'

'You see, the boot's very much on the other foot now, isn't it?' she fired back. 'No, of course

I'm not in love with Mark, but you don't like the idea, do you?'

'Of course, I don't—you're my wife.' Dawning comprehension slivered through Cristo and his shrewd gaze veiled but he remained stubbornly silent, wary as he was of setting her temper off again.

'No wife would want to hear that her husband *ever* loved another woman,' Belle pointed out with dignity. 'It's not personal, it's simply a matter of what's…what's…acceptable. You're my husband. I'm possessive about you. I can't help that.'

'We're both possessive by nature, *bella mia*,' Cristo husked, relieved that the storm had been weathered and she appeared to be calming down.

But Belle was simply putting on an act to save face. She had her pride. She didn't want him to know how she felt about him. Determined to act normally, she shone a light smile of acceptance in his direction before returning to her own room where her clothes were still kept.

While she dressed for lunch, she concentrated her rushing thoughts on the knowledge that her family were arriving within hours. Family, that was what *really* mattered. There was absolutely no point in tearing herself apart over what went on in Cristo's dark, complex head because she couldn't change that.

No doubt, though, he had Betsy on a pedestal. Betsy would always be the unattainable perfect woman in his eyes while Belle would have to settle for being the much more convenient, accessible and real-world wife, who would dutifully help him raise their orphaned brothers and sisters. Well, she could live with that unromantic reality, couldn't she? Of course she could, she told herself urgently, while in the back of her mind furious objections flared. It wasn't a matter of being second-best, she told herself. That was a degrading label and she would go insane if she started picturing herself as some kind of martyr.

Keep it simple, she urged herself sternly. She loved her husband. How had that happened?

She had once been so afraid of falling in love and getting hurt, yet miraculously those concerns had been overwhelmed by the powerful emotions Cristo drummed up inside her. He was very generous, very attentive and absolutely breathtaking in bed. What's not to like, she asked herself accusingly. To want or expect more than she was already getting was downright greedy. He couldn't help what he felt. She should respect his privacy, she reasoned in an even more frantic loop of planning; she shouldn't concern herself with his emotions. And telling him that he was never to see or even speak to Betsy again would not be a winning move...*would it*?

Cristo watched Belle across the lunch table, utterly distrusting her demure expression as she fed Franco from her own plate, breaking her own rules and using the child as a distraction every time Cristo spoke. Franco, of course, lapped up the extra attention and would throw a merry tantrum the next time he was refused a selection from someone else's plate. Cristo was torn between a strong desire to shake Belle and an even stronger desire to drag her back to bed and stamp her as *his* again. Suspecting that he might strike out in that field, he decided to throw in the towel. Belle was in a mood and she would get over it but he was exasperated by the way she was behaving and the wedge she was driving between them. His chair scraped across the terrace tiles as he pushed it back and plunged upright.

'I have a couple of calls to make. I'll see you later,' he said drily.

Targeted by shrewd dark-as-night eyes, Belle went pink and then parted her lips. 'I was planning to sleep in my own room tonight. If the article is to be published tomorrow, I want to be really rested so that I can be with my family,' she muttered uncomfortably.

Cristo gritted his perfect white teeth. It wasn't as if he kept her up *all* night *every* night! Was he a little too demanding in the bedroom? Wouldn't she have complained before now? Belle was no human sacrifice and indeed had

a whole repertoire of delightful approaches calculated to wake him up hot and hard at dawn.
It was an unfortunate recollection when every
basic instinct he possessed craved a renewal
of the very physical connection they shared.
Handsome mouth set in a steely stubborn line,
Cristo strode away.

'Now Cristo's annoyed with me,' Belle mumbled into Franco's tousled hair as he sat on her
lap. 'He never says anything. He just gives me
this sardonic look and it makes me cross and it
makes me sad and for some peculiar reason it
makes me want to run after him and say sorry.'

'*Kiss-do*,' Franco slotted with emphasis into
that confused flood of confidence and the little boy began wriggling off her lap, suddenly
keen to be free.

Belle watched her brother race after Cristo
and her mouth down-curved; it promised to be
a long and lonely afternoon.

In the echoing hall of the palazzo, Tag leapt
straight out of his travel box and flung himself

in a passionate welcome at Belle, pink tongue lolling, ragged tail wagging like mad, his little white and black body wriggling frantically. No sooner had he achieved that reunion and more than a few hugs of reciprocal affection, he glanced at Cristo and growled long and low in his throat.

'*No*, Tag!' Bruno stepped forward to say forcefully, casting his older sister a look of reproach as he scooped up the little dog and walked to the door with him to let him out to run off his over-excitement. Pietro and Lucia, the eight-year-olds too wound up to stay still after hours of travelling confinement, hurtled back outside in the dog's wake. 'You have to be very firm with him, Belle. He doesn't understand anything else.'

'She's the same with Franco,' Cristo remarked wryly. 'Lets him get away with murder.'

'Well, thank you both for that vote of confidence,' Belle countered as her grandmother laughed and folded her into a warm hug. 'How have you been, Gran?'

'I missed you,' Isa confided, her shrewd gaze searching her granddaughter's pale face and shadowed eyes with a frown. 'Missed that little scamp, Franco, as well. We all did.'

'Bruno says there's no shops near here.' Donetta sighed, her pretty face troubled and self-pitying. 'And I've got nothing to wear in this heat.'

'We'll go shopping,' Cristo promised.

'Well, don't expect me to come, especially not if Lucia is going as well.' Bruno winced and shot Cristo a rueful look. 'Lucia only likes the colour pink and won't wear anything else. Getting her into a school uniform will be a nightmare.'

'It's only a phase. She'll get over it,' Belle told him soothingly.

'Mum never did,' Bruno reminded her wryly, his mobile face shadowing with a sudden stark grief that he couldn't hide and which made him hurriedly study the floor with fixed attention.

Belle tensed and tried and failed to think of something comforting to say. Isa grabbed her hand to draw her attention back to her. 'You can start the official tour by showing me to my room,' she suggested. 'And a cup of tea would be even more welcome.'

Isa was tireless in the questions she asked about the Palazzo Maddalena and astonished to be told that Cristo's aristocratic mother didn't care for her former family home.

'The princess grew up here and much prefers life in the city,' Belle explained. 'Cristo only comes here for the occasional holiday so the place does need updating, but I don't like to wade in and start talking about changes when we're only just married.'

'You sounded so happy when you phoned me ,' Isa remarked thoughtfully as she sank with an appreciative sigh into a comfortable wicker armchair on the terrace and reached for the tea Umberto had brought. 'What's happened since then?'

Belle forced a smile. 'Nothing,' she swore with determination. 'I am very happy with Cristo.'

'A man and a woman can find it a challenge

to live together at first,' Isa commented gently. 'Being part of a couple entails compromise.'

'Cristo is really, really good to me,' Belle muttered in a rush, keen to settle any concerns her grandmother might be cherishing. 'I really do have nothing to complain about.'

'Then why aren't you happy?' Isa prompted bluntly. 'I can see something's not right.'

'But it's not something I can discuss... It's something I need to talk about with Cristo,' Belle declared, recognising in that moment that she had actually spoken the truth. Much as she would like to, she could not avoid the subject of Betsy. That had to be discussed and she had to come to terms with it, she registered unhappily. The worst possible stance she could take would be to hold Cristo's feelings against him and poison every other part of their relationship with her bitterness. But it was so very hard to suppress the resentment, jealousy and hurt bubbling up inside her every time she looked at him.

'That sounds sensible,' her grandmother commented with approval and deftly changed the subject to bring Belle up to date on what had been happening in her family since her wedding.

Dinner was served out on the terrace at a big table Umberto had retrieved from a storeroom. The meal was an uproarious affair with all the children talking together, exchanging insults, pulling faces at Franco's table manners, and Belle could see that Cristo was disconcerted by the sheer liveliness of their over-excited siblings. Pietro and Lucia could barely spare the time to eat before they, with Tag in hot pursuit, chased off to explore the gardens again, with Franco trying desperately to keep up with them and breaking down into floods of tears when he was left behind. Cristo went to retrieve the toddler left sobbing at the top of the steps.

'Time for bed, I think,' he murmured quietly. 'I'll call Teresa.'

'No, I'll take him up,' Belle interposed, holding out her arms to take her little brother. 'A bath will soothe him.'

'I'll carry him,' Cristo countered flatly, stunning dark eyes hard and challenging as he studied her set face. 'I'll be back down in—'

'Oh, don't worry about us,' Isa cut in hastily, glancing at Bruno and Donetta. 'The three of us have a date with the television Umberto has most kindly set up for our use.'

Belle stomped upstairs in Cristo's wake, wondering what was wrong with him, her face still burning from that hard, impatient look he had angled at her.

Teresa greeted them on the landing and lifted Franco from her employer's arms. 'Poor little pet…he's exhausted. I'll put him straight in the bath,' she announced.

Belle turned on her heel but a strong tanned hand closed round her forearm to prevent her hurrying back downstairs. 'I'd like a word in private,' Cristo breathed.

Temper sparking fast in the strained mood she was in, Belle rounded on him, her green eyes flashing a fiery warning. 'What on earth is the matter with you?' she hissed.

'You've been avoiding me and ignoring me since this morning,' Cristo pointed out.

Belle's face flamed. 'I'm only trying to keep things polite for the family's benefit.'

'Then you can't act worth a damn,' Cristo told her succinctly, his hand on her forearm sliding down to engulf her fingers instead in a firm grip as he dragged her down the corridor with him. 'And we need to clear the air.'

'I don't want to talk…I'm not ready yet,' Belle exclaimed with more honesty than she had intended, because she had not yet reached the desirable stage where she could consider his feelings for Betsy without raging resentment infiltrating her every thought and reaction.

'Too bad. I'm ready now,' Cristo decreed, shoving wide the door of his bedroom and urging her in ahead of him.

'Is that why you're suddenly acting like a cave man?' Belle demanded furiously.

'No, that's entirely your fault,' Cristo fielded without hesitation. 'If you want to argue with me, argue with me, don't go all passive-aggressive and do it from behind a fake smile.'

'That is not what I've been doing!' Belle protested angrily.

'That's exactly what you've been doing and I've had enough of it. I made the mistake of admitting that at one stage I thought that I had fallen for Betsy—'

'No, you said you *had* fallen for her!' Belle contradicted.

'You mustn't have been listening,' Cristo told her severely. 'For a while before I met you I did believe I'd fallen for her, but once I met you I soon realised that I'd misconstrued my response to her.'

Belle abandoned her angry pacing round the room and fell still. *'Misunderstood?'* she questioned sharply, turning her head back to look at his darkly handsome face.

His lean, strong features taut, Cristo expelled his breath in a rueful hiss. 'You have to understand how I felt at the time Nik and Betsy's marriage broke down. I felt unbearably guilty and accountable because—'

'You told some secret of Nik's to Zarif and he talked when he shouldn't have and let the cat out of the bag,' Belle interposed impatiently. 'Yes, I remember—'

'And Betsy was devastated and she turned to me as Nik's brother, believing that I might know or understand why Nik had done what he had done. That was why she came to me. Unfortunately I didn't know or understand, and I couldn't help, but I felt extremely sorry for her. For whatever reasons, Nik had treated her badly. I felt very protective towards her and angry with Nik and I honestly assumed that those feelings were love.'

While she listened to what Cristo had to say, Belle was slowly breaking out in a cold sweat of relief because she was finally recognising that somehow in her hot-headed emotional response she had got the wrong end of the stick. Cristo had misinterpreted his feelings for Betsy and then recognised his mistake. Belle could understand how confused Cristo must've felt at the time, torn between guilt and responsibility for his brother's marriage breakdown while feeling both disloyal to his brother and strongly sympathetic towards Betsy's plight.

'I can understand that. You felt responsible so you tried to be helpful and provide a supportive shoulder.'

'I did still think I loved her when I asked you to marry me even though I'd never been attracted to Betsy the way I was to you,' Cristo admitted with a twist of his mouth. 'That sounds ludicrously naïve, doesn't it?'

Belle was frowning in surprise. 'You *weren't* attracted to her?'

'No. I assumed that was because I still thought of her as my brother's wife but I think it was more because she wasn't my type and didn't appeal to me on that level.'

'But…I've seen photos of her and she's incredibly pretty!' Belle fired back at him in ridiculous challenge.

'I've discovered that tall, curvy redheads

are much more my style, *amata mia*,' Cristo quipped. 'Particularly ones who can give as good as they get in a row and can function as my intellectual equal.'

Belle dragged in a steadying breath before she could ask uncertainly, 'Are you talking about me?'

'Who else?' Dark golden eyes locked to her bemused face and lingered. 'After all, it was only because I fell in love with you that I learned to appreciate that I'd *never* been in love with Betsy.'

Mouth running dry, eyes wide, Belle was suddenly feeling very short of breath and even slightly dizzy, as if the floor below her feet were rocking. And indeed it might as well have been because it seemed that most of her pessimistic assumptions had been glaringly wrong. 'You fell in love with me?'

'And it was almost love at first sight,' Cristo teased with a charismatic smile. 'Before you decided to try and convince me that you were your mother and a forty-odd-year-old woman,

I saw you crossing the lawn, wearing a pair of shorts, and you have curves and legs to die for,' Cristo told her with a wicked grin.

'You're so superficial,' Belle mumbled in a pained tone of amusement. So superficial but *mine*, she was thinking lovingly.

'Not at all. I love your legs but I love your brain and your ready tongue more,' Cristo confided without hesitation. 'In fact there's a whole host of things I like about you that have nothing to do with your very sexy appearance.'

'Like...?' Belle pressed shamelessly.

'Your loyalty and love for your family, your kindness, your lack of greed,' Cristo enumerated, moving closer step by step while Belle continued to survey him with wonder. He loved her, not Betsy, and her brain was struggling to process that alien conviction. She was not second-best; she was his *first* choice and he genuinely cared about her. The first heady spur of joy surged through her like a rejuvenating drug.

'I like lots of things about you too,' Belle burbled. 'But I fell in love with you without knowing I was doing it. It was only when I thought you loved Betsy that I realised how I felt about you.'

'Great minds think alike,' Cristo purred, stroking the side of her face with a gentle forefinger. 'You love me, I love you. We're a perfect match.'

'No, we're imperfect but that's okay…we're only human,' Belle mumbled unsteadily, her heart leaping behind her breastbone as Cristo drew her into his arms and eased her wonderfully, reassuringly close to his lean, powerful frame. 'Oh, I can't believe this…I was *so* miserable today!'

'I would've told you how I felt about you then if you hadn't been so angry I was afraid that you wouldn't believe me,' Cristo confessed. 'Let's face it, neither of us was looking for or expecting love in this marriage, but you turned out to be the best thing that's ever happened to me and I think the family we already have will be the icing on the cake.'

Belle dealt him an anxious upward glance,

afraid he was being too optimistic in his out-look. 'But you can get lots of little problems too with family.'

'And together we'll deal with them,' Cristo asserted huskily as he brushed his mouth very tenderly over hers, lifting his handsome dark head to stare down at her with tender love and appreciation softening his stunning gaze. 'You're mine, my love, my wife, my future…'

'I like the sound of that very much,' Belle ad-mitted, snuggling into his broad chest with a happy sigh. 'But you know when you said that it wouldn't be worth my while learning Ital-ian, I assumed you only saw me as a short-term prospect.'

'*Ma no*…certainly not,' Cristo chided huskily. 'I only meant that these days I don't spend a lot of time in Italy.'

'I'd still like to learn.'

'I love you,' he told her in Italian and she re-peated the words faithfully back with a little giggle as he backed her down on the bed with a clear agenda in mind.

* * *

Belle greeted her family with a shining smile the following morning. Isa beamed and said nothing. Franco was scolded for trying to steal off Cristo's plate and Tag for snarling at Cristo's ankles. Pietro and Lucia squabbled as usual. Donetta wanted to know when they were going shopping and Bruno was making rapturous comments about the quality of the light.

Below the level of the table, Cristo gripped Belle's hand in his and breathed, 'Family is what it's all about, *amata mia*. My father missed out on so much.'

EPILOGUE

FOUR YEARS LATER, Belle stood at a cheval mirror and pulled her stretchy dress away from the very small bump she sported.

'You're pregnant. You're supposed to be that shape,' her grandmother told her reprovingly.

'I'm putting on a lot of weight though,' Belle groused, checking the generous curve of her bust and hips in the mirror as she turned round and pulled a face.

'Not too much,' Isa contradicted. 'You're very active and naturally you need to eat. At least you're not as sick as your mother was when she was expecting.'

'There is that,' Belle conceded reluctantly. 'Now, are you sure you're going to be all right while we're away?'

'Belle, you and Cristo will only be away for

five days, of course we'll be all right,' the older woman declared lightly. 'Stop fussing.'

Cristo and Belle were celebrating their fourth wedding anniversary in Venice where they would be visiting the princess and Henri in their palazzo on the Grand Canal but staying in a small intimate hotel that Cristo had carefully selected for them. Belle could barely credit that so much time had passed since their wedding and that soon she would be a mother in her own right.

Cristo had bought a fabulous house for them in Holland Park. Bruno was now studying art at college and Donetta was planning to do fashion design. Pietro and Lucia were both in secondary school and fought a little less often now that they were so conscious of being almost teenagers. Franco was a sturdy six-year-old in primary school, who insisted on having his curls cropped the minute they became visible and who modelled his every masculine move on Cristo, whom in common with the twins he called, 'Dad.'

Although they had started out with a ready-made family, who had been officially adopted by Cristo and Belle within months of their first wedding, Cristo had never overlooked their personal relationship or taken it for granted. They had, after all and at his insistence, had their marriage blessed in an Italian church service shortly before the first Christmas they had shared, both of them feeling the need to exchange their vows with rather more sincerity and emotion than had figured when they had initially married. They also enjoyed regular weekend breaks and holidays as a couple.

It had been during their last romantic break that Cristo had admitted that he would love her to have his child. That development had taken place far sooner than either of them had expected because Belle had fallen pregnant within a month of that decision. She smiled, hand splaying across her tummy as she thought of the little girl on the way to joining the Ravelli family. She could hardly wait and her brothers and sisters were equally excited at the new addition in the offing.

Indeed, Belle was happier than she had ever dreamt of being with Cristo and her family. And she had never been so busy. The palazzo, where they usually spent their summers on a family holiday, had been modernised. The whole family circle had drawn closer. Cristo's brother, Nik Christakis, still intimidated Belle but his life had taken some surprising turns since their first meeting and he had definitely warmed up from the driven workaholic he had once been.

Zarif's life was still a story under development and Belle loved visiting Vashir with its colourful vibrant culture and fabulous history. Cristo's younger brother had weathered the storms over the scandal of his father's secret double life because the rumours about Gaetano's misbehaviour had once been so wild that the truth was no more shocking to the populace, who could only marvel that Zarif was such a conservative male in comparison.

Belle clambered into the limo that was to

whisk her to the airport to meet Cristo and smiled, looking forward to the promise of having her husband's undivided attention for a few days. An hour and half later, she boarded the private jet, her attention switching straight to Cristo's tall, well-built figure as he pushed aside his laptop and sprang upright to greet her in the aisle.

'You look beautiful, *amata mia*,' he told her huskily.

Belle slid self-mocking hands down over her bust and hips and quipped, 'Well, you are getting a more generous portion of me with every month that goes past...'

'And I *love* it,' Cristo growled, bending down to kiss her ripe peach-tinted mouth with hungry appreciation. 'I think you look incredibly sexy.'

'Tell me more,' she urged as he settled her down in a comfortable seat beside his and fastened her belt for take-off.

'Later. Right now it's time for this...' Cristo slowly slid an emerald ring onto her wedding finger. 'It's the same colour as your eyes and it is to signify my gratitude and appreciation for four very happy years of marriage.'

'Thank you, it's absolutely gorgeous. Unfortunately my gift is unavailable right at this moment, so you'll have to wait.'

'What is it?' Cristo asked curiously.

'Well, it might be turquoise and frilly and exactly the sort of thing you like but you'll just have to wait and see,' she warned him with an irreverent grin. 'It has to be love, Cristo. It really has to be love I feel for you.'

'I adore you, *amata mia*,' Cristo murmured, holding her hand in his. 'And if you're talking about what I think you are, I can hardly wait.'

Belle rolled her green eyes teasingly and her colour heightened. 'You don't have to wait. I'm wearing it. Have you ever heard of the Mile High Club?'

* * * * *

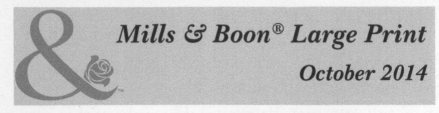

Mills & Boon® Large Print
October 2014

RAVELLI'S DEFIANT BRIDE
Lynne Graham

WHEN DA SILVA BREAKS THE RULES
Abby Green

THE HEARTBREAKER PRINCE
Kim Lawrence

THE MAN SHE CAN'T FORGET
Maggie Cox

A QUESTION OF HONOUR
Kate Walker

WHAT THE GREEK CAN'T RESIST
Maya Blake

AN HEIR TO BIND THEM
Dani Collins

BECOMING THE PRINCE'S WIFE
Rebecca Winters

NINE MONTHS TO CHANGE HIS LIFE
Marion Lennox

TAMING HER ITALIAN BOSS
Fiona Harper

SUMMER WITH THE MILLIONAIRE
Jessica Gilmore

0914 Rom LP

Mills & Boon® Large Print
November 2014

CHRISTAKIS'S REBELLIOUS WIFE
Lynne Graham

AT NO MAN'S COMMAND
Melanie Milburne

CARRYING THE SHEIKH'S HEIR
Lynn Raye Harris

BOUND BY THE ITALIAN'S CONTRACT
Janette Kenny

DANTE'S UNEXPECTED LEGACY
Catherine George

A DEAL WITH DEMAKIS
Tara Pammi

THE ULTIMATE PLAYBOY
Maya Blake

HER IRRESISTIBLE PROTECTOR
Michelle Douglas

THE MAVERICK MILLIONAIRE
Alison Roberts

THE RETURN OF THE REBEL
Jennifer Faye

THE TYCOON AND THE WEDDING PLANNER
Kandy Shepherd

MILLS & BOON®

Why shop at millsandboon.co.uk?

Each year, thousands of romance readers find their perfect read at millsandboon.co.uk. That's because we're passionate about bringing you the very best romantic fiction. Here are some of the advantages of shopping at www.millsandboon.co.uk:

* **Get new books first**—you'll be able to buy your favourite books one month before they hit the shops

* **Get exclusive discounts**—you'll also be able to buy our specially created monthly collections, with up to 50% off the RRP

* **Find your favourite authors**—latest news, interviews and new releases for all your favourite authors and series on our website, plus ideas for what to try next

* **Join in**—once you've bought your favourite books, don't forget to register with us to rate, review and join in the discussions

Visit **www.millsandboon.co.uk**
for all this and more today!